FUGITIVE JUSTICE

Rayven T. Hill

Ray of Joy Publishing
Toronto

Books by Rayven T. Hill
Blood and Justice
Cold Justice
Justice for Hire
Captive Justice
Justice Overdue
Justice Returns
Personal Justice
Silent Justice
Web of Justice
Fugitive Justice
Profane Justice

Visit rayventhill.com for more information
on these and future releases.

This book is a work of fiction. Names, characters, places,
businesses, organizations, events and incidents either are the
product of the author's imagination or are used fictitiously.
Any resemblance to actual persons, living or dead, events or
locales is entirely coincidental.

Published by Ray of Joy Publishing
Toronto

ISBN-13: 978-0-9947781-8-5

FUGITIVE JUSTICE

CHAPTER 1

DAY 1 - Monday, 4:42 p.m.

THIS WAS GONNA BE a breeze. All it would take is five minutes of his time, and he'd be an unknown amount of dollars richer—a hundred bucks or a thousand bucks, it was good enough for him.

Anything that helped him avoid putting in long hours at a dead-end job to collect a measly paycheck was a good thing. He didn't have expensive tastes, and that's why this latest brilliant idea of his was right up his alley.

He checked his pistol to make sure it was ready to go. It was. He didn't intend to use the weapon unless necessary; it was just for show—to guarantee they took him seriously. It wasn't that he had any qualms about it, but he'd never killed anyone in front of witnesses before. That kind of thing could have serious consequences.

He turned up his collar, then removed a black ski mask from his jacket pocket and pulled it over his short hair, tugging it down over his face. After a careful glance around to make sure no one was nearby, he stepped out of the alley and onto the sidewalk.

He took three quick strides and paused for half a second, then, with a gloved hand, pulled open the tempered-glass door that led into Commerce Bank.

It was near closing time, and he knew from experience the bank would be almost deserted at this hour of the day. And he was correct. There were no customers. Two teller windows had their "Welcome" signs on display, no doubt waiting for last minute stragglers. He chose the nearest one.

A young girl stood behind the counter, her head slightly down. She worked at a piece of gum, her jaw keeping tempo with the rhythmic tapping of her long fake fingernails on a keyboard in front of her.

He hurried forward, slipped the gun from his jacket pocket, and laid it on the counter with a soft clunk. A finger massaged the trigger as he leaned in to speak.

"Be with you in a moment," she said in a bored voice without looking up.

He leaned closer and spoke in a hushed tone. "This is a stickup. Gimme all the money in your till."

Her jaw stopped working, her fingers paused mid-stroke, and her eyes turned upward. Her well-chewed gum lay forgotten on her tongue as her mouth fell open.

She glanced left and right.

"Look at me," he said.

She looked at him, her frightened eyes widening.

"What's the matter?" he whispered, the ski mask hiding a

2

frown. "You've never been robbed before? You're supposed to give me the money."

She stared at him.

He tapped the barrel of the gun on the counter.

She blinked twice, then eyed the weapon and slipped the money drawer open. "There ... there's not much," she managed to say.

"It's okay. Gimme what's there. And don't press any alarm, or I'll shoot you."

Her hands shook as she removed a stack of money from the drawer. From where he stood, the bills looked like fifties. She set them in front of her, then withdrew a small bundle of hundreds and laid them on the pile. Next came the twenties.

"Forget the rest," he said. "That'll do."

This was taking more time than he'd expected. He glanced at the other teller. She was leaning in to her computer, no doubt doing her daily totals, anxious to clean it up and get home to her two cats and her lazy boyfriend.

The teller fumbled with the pile of bills, and time was passing. He knew the surveillance cameras would be catching his every move, and he had to get out of there before somebody glanced at the monitor.

She managed to pick up the small pile of money with a trembling hand. She set the stack in front of him, then shrank back and watched him, her hands clasped together above her waist.

He scooped up the bills, jammed them into his jacket pocket, and turned away from the counter. He paused as a woman who looked like she might be the manager crossed the floor toward him. She stopped short, and her eyes bulged when he raised the pistol and pointed it at her.

"Stay there," he said, waving the weapon. The manager raised her hands chest-high, and he turned and dashed toward the exit.

The door opened outward and a woman bustled in, a bag of groceries in one hand, her handbag over her other shoulder. She stopped inside the doorway, caught by surprise as he rushed toward her. Then a hand went to her mouth, and she inhaled a sharp breath, her bug eyes on his pistol as the door swung shut at her heels.

A man's voice shouted from behind him, "Stop right there. Put the gun down."

He glanced back. It was a security guard. And he had a weapon drawn. Where'd he come from? As far as he knew, this bank had never employed a guard before. And where was the guy when he came in? Probably on break. Or maybe he'd seen the robbery going down on a monitor in his little hideaway closet somewhere and decided to play the hero.

Either way, it was too late to stop him now. He disregarded the guard, elbowed the woman aside, and pushed the door.

It wouldn't open.

He rammed it with his shoulder. It groaned and held. Panicking now, he kicked at the glass. No luck. Someone had sprung an alarm and it must've automatically locked the doors. He kicked the door again, then again and again until his toes were sore, his soft running shoes no match for the tempered glass.

"Drop the gun," the guard yelled from a safe distance.

Spinning back around, he grabbed the startled woman from behind, his arm around her waist, and pointed the weapon at her head. He glared at the guard. "Open the door or I'll shoot her."

The guard lowered his weapon halfway and gave a bewildered stare. He obviously had no idea what to do. This was probably the first time he'd ever witnessed a robbery, and he'd likely never even been this close to one before.

"Unlock the door," the robber shouted. "Or she gets it."

The guard licked his lips, shuffled his feet, and continued to stare.

The hostage trembled all over. "Please," she said to the guard, her voice quivering in fear. "Open the door for him."

This was getting nuts. He hadn't counted on any of this happening, and he didn't wanna kill the woman. She wasn't much good dead—she was his passage out of here.

But if someone didn't open the door soon, he'd have to make good on his threat and kill her. At well over six feet tall, and a body built to match, he had enough strength in his muscled arms to break the woman's neck with his bare hands, if necessary. That would keep the sound of a gunshot from attracting unwanted attention.

But then, he'd be sunk without a hostage, and he'd have to find another one.

Maybe there was another way out of here. A back door, perhaps.

He looked around frantically, his eyes stopping at the rear of the room. A woman crouched behind a desk in a glass-walled cubicle. All that was visible was the top of her head and her widened eyes as she watched the events take place.

The manager had backed up to the wall, her hands still obediently in the air. The two tellers had ducked down behind the counter, and the guard still stared like a dimwit.

The bank robber muttered a long string of curses at the stupidity of everyone around him. Why wouldn't they open the door?

Abruptly recovering from his trance, the guard holstered his weapon, then reached to his belt and fiddled with a ring of keys.

The dumb guard had finally realized a woman's life was worth a little more than a lousy stack of money.

The robber stepped back as the guard ambled forward, still playing around with the keys in his shaking hands. He selected one, held it up, and moved toward the door.

The guard slipped the key into the lock, keeping one uneasy eye on the robber. He fidgeted with the key, gave it a turn, then stepped back.

Finally.

The robber let go of the woman and spun toward the door.

Without warning, the guard moved in, one hand reaching for the robber's weapon, the other tugging the mask down over his eyes. It pulled him off balance and disoriented him, and he couldn't see.

He managed to hold on to his gun, and he swung the other arm toward his attacker. He missed. He made a fist and swung again, only managing to whack his own hand against the wall, sending a ripple of pain up his arm.

While fumbling to find the door, he struggled with his free hand to work the mask into place. A sudden blow to the side of his head stunned him. He recovered and adjusted the mask again, but he still couldn't see, and where was the door? The guard was gonna beat him into the ground if he didn't do something and do it soon.

Desperate now, he pulled the mask off, let go of the woman, and swung his pistol hand toward the guard. The butt of the weapon connected with the side of the guard's head, knocking him to a groaning heap on the floor.

The guard hadn't seen his face, but there were cameras all around, and he was pretty sure everything was being recorded. He had to keep his head down and get out of there as fast as possible.

He jammed the mask into his pocket and turned to leave. Too late. His hostage had stepped back, her hand to her mouth, and her startled eyes looked up into his exposed face.

He stared back, his mind running at lightning speed through the current state of events.

And the current state of events told him he was screwed.

Unless …

He looked at the guard on the floor, then at the woman in the cubicle as she peeked out from behind her desk. Both she and the manager were too far away to recognize him again, but the hostage was a different story.

He raised the pistol and sighed, then mumbled, "Sorry," and shot her in the head.

Five seconds later, he was running down the alley, the faint sound of sirens coming from far away. He cursed his luck and wondered how his wonderful plan had gone so wrong.

CHAPTER 2

Monday, 5:35 p.m.

ANNIE LINCOLN slipped a sheet of freshly baked buns onto a cooling rack and was pulling off her oven mitts when the doorbell rang. She finger-combed her midlength blond hair into place, then took off her apron and hurried to answer the door.

When she opened it, a cop stood outside, a big grin on his face. Except, right now he wasn't a cop, and he wasn't Detective Hank Corning, homicide detective.

He was just Hank, and he was early for dinner.

"Hi, Hank," Annie said. She smiled at the tall woman beside him. "It's nice to see you again, Amelia."

"Thanks for having us over," Amelia said. "Hank's told me a lot about your cooking."

Annie laughed. "I've heard about Hank's cooking, and compared to it, anything would be better." She motioned for the visitors to come in and herded them into the living room.

Amelia took a seat on the couch under the window and crossed her legs. At thirty-eight years old, with long blond hair and smiling blue eyes, she was remarkably beautiful. The large sum of money her husband had left when he'd died a few years ago hadn't changed her. Though she'd been used to big money all her life, she still retained the small-town, girl-next-door attitude that'd caught Hank's heart.

The two had met several months ago on a case Hank had been working on with the Lincolns, and they'd hit it off almost from the first glance.

Hank ran a hand through his short-cropped hair and dropped his six-foot frame down beside Amelia. Though he was good-looking and always a gentleman, in contrast to her, he was just an ordinary guy who lived in an ordinary apartment and was broke most of the time.

In Annie's opinion, the two were a perfect couple. She settled into her easy chair and wondered what was taking Hank so long to pop the question.

Hank dropped an arm on the back of the couch. "I didn't see the Firebird. Is Jake here?"

"He should be back soon," Annie said, glancing at her watch. "His car's in the garage and he took mine. He's on a stakeout, but he said he'd be home before six."

Though Annie knew stakeouts were Jake's least favorite chore, they were an important part of the vocation she and her husband had chosen.

Not so long ago, Jake had been a construction engineer for one of Canada's largest land developers. At the time, Annie had been doing part-time research for a variety of companies from her home office. When the business Jake worked for had gotten into financial difficulties, he'd been laid off.

He'd moped around the house a few weeks, then one day approached Annie with the idea of expanding her growing business and taking on the name of Lincoln Investigations. Annie had decided it wouldn't hurt to give it a whirl.

Their new venture had required they take the proper course, get PI licenses, and pass police background checks. Several weeks later, they'd designed and printed new letterhead, gotten a dedicated phone line, and proudly displayed their diplomas on the office wall.

Lincoln Investigations had been born.

Though routine searches for missing persons, background checks for businesses, and research for legal firms were still their mainstays, they'd found themselves involved in several high-profile cases. Dangerous people of all kinds had crossed their paths. With the help of their growing relationship with RHPD, Lincoln Investigations had successfully tracked down some of Richmond Hill's worst criminals.

"Looks like you have a visitor," Hank said, glancing out the front window. "Somebody in a white Corolla."

Annie laughed, a twinkle in her eye. "That's Jake, and he's driving my new car."

Hank raised his brows and looked at Annie with deep brown eyes. "You got a new car?"

"Yup. Picked it up this morning."

"It's about time. That old Escort must've been on its last legs."

Annie chuckled. "Jake took good care of it. It's got some miles left in it yet. I'm sure the new owner will appreciate it a few more years."

The front door rattled, then closed. "Saw your Chevy out front, Hank," Jake called from the foyer. "Figured you'd be here by now."

Annie turned her head as a six-foot-four-inch man came into the room and leaned against the doorframe. He had a crooked grin on his face, and once again, Annie couldn't help but notice her husband was the best-looking guy she'd ever seen. And thanks to his intense daily workout, he had a body to match.

"Heard you were on a stakeout," Hank said.

"Yeah, but nothing came of it," Jake said with a shrug. "Some guy said his wife was picking up men in bars every day while he was at work. I followed the woman to the mall, to a friend's house, then to a bakery before she went home. If she's having an affair, I can't figure out how."

"Maybe she's taking a day off," Hank said with a chuckle.

"I think the guy's paranoid," Jake said. "She's about twenty and he's in his forties. Nothing wrong with that, but perhaps he feels insecure." He shrugged. "Who knows? I'll keep at it until he's satisfied. As long as he's willing to pay."

"Hey, Uncle Hank." A four-foot-tall bundle of energy charged into the room and ran to the cop.

Hank grinned and leaned forward, giving the eight-year-old arrival a fist bump. "Hey, Matty. It's great to see you."

Matty stood back and gave Amelia a polite, shy smile, then dropped to the floor and sat cross-legged, leaning against the wall.

A quiet ringing sound filled the room.

"It's mine," Hank said, reaching for his inner pocket. He pulled out his cell phone and had a brief conversation, then put his phone away and sighed.

Amelia looked at him, a quizzical look on her face. "They need you?"

Hank nodded and blew out a long breath. "There's been a bank robbery at Commerce Bank. The robber escaped, but not before killing a hostage." He shrugged and moved forward, sitting on the edge of the couch, and gave Annie an apologetic look. "I gotta go. Sorry, Annie."

"Duty calls," Annie said as she stood.

"Sure, but I was looking forward to a nice home-cooked meal. Now I'll have to settle for a quick burger on the way there, and probably won't get home until after midnight."

"I'll drop Amelia home later," Jake said. "And now you know why I didn't wanna be a cop."

Jake and Hank had become friends early in their high school years, and during that time, the duo had become an inseparable trio when Jake had discovered Annie. After high school, Hank had hoped Jake would go to the police academy with him and become a cop. For some reason, Jake had been more partial to Annie, and had elected to go to University of Toronto along with her.

Their friendship had endured, and Annie was pleased to add another female to the group of friends. Amelia fit right in.

Hank stood and helped his girlfriend to her feet, and she and Annie saw the cop to the door. After giving Amelia a quick kiss, he dropped her hand and stepped outside.

"We'll do this again as soon as you can," Annie said.

Hank glanced back and nodded in agreement, then waved a hand and hurried to his car.

Annie watched the detective drive away. He was in for a long night.

CHAPTER 3

Monday, 6:16 p.m.

HANK MADE A CALL to Detective Simon King on his way to the crime scene. His occasional partner was filling his face at a fast-food joint near his apartment, and he told Hank he'd meet him at the bank as soon as possible.

Though it occasionally took King a while to get moving, with the proper nudge, he was reasonably dependable. In fact, King had already arrived and was climbing from his vehicle when Hank reached the scene and pulled in beside his partner's car.

King slammed his door, tugged his t-shirt into place, and tucked a hand into a pocket of his faded jeans. The cop looked pretty much the way he normally did. Long greasy hair dripped down from under a faded baseball cap. Three days' growth of beard decorated his lean face. The badge fastened to his belt was the only way anyone could identify him as a cop.

King had originally been a narc, but a few months ago, for reasons not shared with Hank, he'd been transferred from Toronto, where he'd spent a lot of time undercover. RHPD was small, and the homicide division even smaller. Captain Diego had seen fit to team up the unlikely pair to tackle the increasing workload as the small Canadian city expanded, and crime grew along with it.

Hank got out of his vehicle and glanced around. Curious passersby lined the street near Commerce Bank, craning their necks to get a better view of what might have gone on inside the building. A handful of officers milled about near the yellow border, making sure none of the inquisitive citizenry breached the barrier.

The CSI van was parked nearby, investigators no doubt documenting the scene in painstaking detail. The coroner's vehicle sat near the front doors of the building, ready to transport an occupied body bag to the medical examiner for further examination.

Hank turned and nodded at King, and the two detectives ducked under the tape and made their way into the front door of the bank.

Directly inside and to their right, the body of a woman lay in an unbecoming position, her handbag still over her shoulder, and a bag of groceries at one side. She lay on her back, one leg twisted unnaturally under the other. A small amount of blood had seeped from an unsightly wound in the middle of her forehead.

No doubt she was the unfortunate hostage, chosen by an uncaring Lady Luck.

Hank had seen a lot of needless death in the fifteen years he'd been a homicide detective. Often the victims had brought on their own deaths by involving themselves with dangerous people. Gang wars and drug wars produced even more bodies. Occasionally, death came by sheer stupidity, or perhaps at the hand of a jealous spouse or lover. But the thing that tore at his heart was when an innocent person found themselves in the wrong place at the wrong time, resulting in their untimely death.

Hank glanced up a couple of inches into the eyes of a tall, gaunt-faced man holding a clipboard in one hand. He was lead investigator Rod Jameson, and he spoke to Hank in a deep drawling voice.

"The vic's name is Arlina Madine," Jameson said. "Fifty-three years old. We haven't tracked down any family yet, but we're working on it."

Hank nodded. "Keep me informed."

"Sure, Hank," Rod said.

Hank crouched down and gazed into the victim's graying face. The appearance of the wound told him she'd been shot at point-blank range, probably from no more than eight or ten inches. The projectile had exited her skull from the rear, and an investigator was in the careful process of extracting it from where it was embedded in the wall between a pair of ATMs.

Perhaps it would tell Hank a story.

"Anyone see the killer's face?" King asked Jameson.

Jameson pointed into the main area of the bank. "Haven't talked to the witnesses yet."

Hank stood and followed King's gaze. Three women occupied comfortable guest chairs lining the wall opposite the teller windows. Hank assumed they were the witnesses, huddled out of the way until their story could be told. A fourth woman, dressed in a smart business suit, paced in a small circle, casting occasional glances toward the newcomers.

"Guess we'd better talk to them and send them home," Hank said. "But I want to view the video first."

Jameson pointed again, this time toward the pacing woman. "She's the manager."

As Hank and King approached the woman, she stopped her nervous pacing and came toward them, introducing herself. Hank asked to see the video, and she led them down a short hallway and into a small room. A block of four monitors was positioned on the wall above a long table, showing a live feed of the inside of the bank from a variety of viewpoints.

A man dressed in a guard's uniform wheeled his chair back from the desk and introduced himself. "I'm Buck," he said, offering a hand.

Hank shook his hand and King nodded.

"I'd like to see the video from the time of the robbery," Hank said.

Buck motioned toward the monitors. "All cued up and ready to go. Four different videos from four different cameras. One outside the front door and three inside."

Hank leaned in as Buck started the first video. It showed a view from the rear of the main room, and they watched the unsettling scene unfold. The robber entered the bank and approached the teller, then the exchange between the killer and Buck took place, resulting in the taking of a hostage. The manager drew a sharp breath as a gunshot sounded and the hostage fell to the floor.

Buck cued up the other videos, one by one, and the group watched the same events over and over again.

Hank pointed to the first video. "That's the only one that catches the whole thing in detail."

"But none of them show more than a partial view of the killer's face," King said.

"We'll go over them all a hundred times if we have to. We'll find something," Hank said and turned to Buck. "I need copies of these videos at once."

Buck grinned and scooped up a flash drive from the desk. "Right here," he said, holding it out.

Hank took the recording and dropped it into his jacket pocket, then turned to King. "You interview the manager, then see what Buck can tell you about the robber. I'll talk to the other witnesses."

Hank returned to the main room and approached the group of women. Two were in their early twenties, one a few years older. He was especially interested in what the teller who had confronted the robber had to say.

He sat on the edge of the only unoccupied chair, introduced himself, then said, "We'll get detailed statements from all of you later, but right now, I have a few questions."

The older woman nodded. The other two remained silent and waited for him to continue.

Hank pulled out a notepad and pen and started by getting the names of the women, jotting the information down.

"Which one of you is the teller?" he asked.

One of the two girls raised a trembling hand. She appeared still shaken from her ordeal, and Hank smiled in an attempt to put her at ease.

"Can you describe his voice?" he asked, leaning in.

"Just a regular voice."

"High-pitched? Deep?"

The girl shook her head. "I ... I was kinda nervous. It sounded normal to me."

Hank smiled again. "What about his eyes? Anything distinguishable about them?"

"They were brown ... I think."

"Was he wearing any jewelry?" Hank asked. "Necklace, rings?"

"Maybe. I ... I mean, I don't know. I didn't notice."

"A watch, perhaps?"

She shrugged.

"What about the way he spoke?" Hank asked. "Did he have an accent, or anything that sticks out as being different?"

She shook her head again.

"What happened after you gave him the money?"

"He left and I hid behind the counter. I didn't see anything after that."

Hank sighed lightly and turned to the other young woman. She was more nervous than the first, and she claimed not to have seen anything useful, unaware of the events taking place until Buck had approached the gunman. She had immediately ducked down behind the counter until it was over.

He looked at the older woman. "Can you tell me anything?"

She motioned toward a glass-walled cubicle not far away. "I was in my office," she said. "I ducked down behind my desk when I saw what was taking place." She paused. "When his mask was pulled off, I saw his face, but not very clearly."

"Do you think you could recognize him again?" Hank asked.

"I … I don't know. He was tall and clean-shaven. Very muscular. And he had short dark hair." She shrugged. "Maybe I could pick him out of a lineup, but he didn't look much different than thousands of other guys."

Hank glanced at the cubicle and then toward the front doors. It was a distance of about twenty-five feet. He turned back to the woman. "This is important. You might be the only one who saw him."

"I only caught a brief glimpse of him," she said. "That's all I can tell you."

Hank handed business cards around, thanked the women, and stood. "If you think of something, please contact me. An officer will take your statements before long."

One of them might remember something after having had a chance to calm down, but right now, he had gotten about all he was going to get from them.

He headed toward the exit. King had returned and was waiting near the front doors, chatting with Jameson. The body of the victim had been removed, and CSI was packing up.

"Get anything?" Hank asked King.

"Robber got away with forty-eight hundred," he said. "The hundreds were marked." King paused and shrugged. "The manager didn't see his face."

"And Buck?"

"Buck had nothing he could tell me that would identify the guy. He never saw his face, either. Said the guy had a swing on him like a gorilla. Knocked him down before he had a chance to do anything."

Unless one of the witnesses remembered something vital, Hank's best chance of identifying the killer would be from the video. Their technical whiz would soon be taking a close look at it, and Hank had high hopes for its usefulness.

King stepped outside and Hank followed. He glanced around, his eyes stopping on the Channel 7 Action News van, further blocking the already slow-moving traffic on Main Street.

He didn't want to waste any time talking to Lisa Krunk right now. He scanned the crowd and spied her cameraman, Don, as he took video of the scene outside the bank. But Lisa was nowhere around. She had to be sticking her long nose in somewhere, and he decided to scram before she tracked him down.

He had nothing he could share right now, anyway. She'd have to wait for an official statement like the rest of the media.

Besides, there was a killer out there somewhere, and it was Hank's sworn duty to bring him in as soon as possible.

CHAPTER 4

DAY 2 - Tuesday, 8:44 a.m.

ANNIE JUMPED WHEN the front door slammed, and she wondered when Matty would ever learn how to close a door properly. He'd rushed from the house and, along with his best friend Kyle from next door, would walk the two blocks to school, as usual.

Jake was in the garage, changing the oil on his car. Again. He kept his 1986 Pontiac Firebird in top shape, and he was always fiddling with something or other out there.

And Annie had the house to herself. At least for a while, she could enjoy a little peace and quiet.

She and Amelia had talked until late last night. Jake had gone to bed, and she'd taken Amelia home and put off straightening up the house until morning. Last night's dinner dishes sat in the sink along with today's breakfast dishes, and though Jake had offered to clean up, she'd declined. Not that he didn't know how to wash a dish or two. He just wasn't that good at it.

Maybe it was a guy thing. Who knows? He could spit-shine the Firebird until it sparkled, but couldn't manage to remove the grease from a kitchen plate. She assumed it was caused by a mental block of some kind, specific to the male of the human species.

She had just dunked her hands in the warm sudsy water when Jake wandered into the house. After washing the grime from his hands, he helped her dry the dishes. He wasn't too bad at that.

Then a ringing sound came from the office.

"That's my cell," Jake said, tossing the towel on the counter. "I wondered where I left that thing."

He strode to the office, and Annie heard him carrying on a conversation. She poured herself a cup of coffee and one for Jake and settled down at the kitchen table.

Today was going to be a lazy day. She had a couple of hours of research to do for a client and, unless something else came up in the meantime, the rest of the day was free.

She wanted to catch up on some of her studies on crime scene technique. Her small library was bulging with unread books, and she was determined to learn as much as possible about all aspects of criminal investigations.

And maybe she'd go for a ride in her new car—just to get the hang of it. They'd only picked it up from the dealership the morning before, and she was aching to get it on the highway.

Jake came into the room, sat at the table, and took a short

sip from his mug. "Looks like I might have to do another stakeout," he said. "Another cheating spouse."

"There's no shortage of those," Annie said, then sighed. "I assume you'll be wanting to use my car."

Jake shrugged. "Not much choice. Mine's too conspicuous for a stakeout."

There went the car ride.

"I have an appointment to meet her at nine thirty, and she wants me to get on it this morning," Jake said. "I have no idea how long I might be. You know how it is with these things."

Annie knew how it was. In the past, Jake had spent anywhere from a few minutes to a few days staking out a variety of places. As long as the client paid, Jake didn't complain all that much. At least it was safer than chasing down killers.

Jake took a long sip of coffee, then set it down and went back to the office. He returned a few minutes later with a sports bag stuffed full of the necessary equipment, including a pair of binoculars and a Nikon digital camera with a powerful zoom lens.

He dropped the bag onto the table, then picked up his coffee and went into the living room. In a moment, the sound of the television could be heard.

Annie put together some sandwiches, tucked them into the bag along with a few bottles of cold water, and sat down to finish her coffee.

"Come here a minute," Jake called from the other room.

He was pointing at the television when Annie joined him

in the living room. "You missed it," he said. "It was a story about the bank robbery last night. I haven't talked to Hank yet today, but according to the reporter, they haven't caught the guy yet."

"Do they know who they're looking for?"

"Apparently not. He wore a mask, and he killed the only person who saw his face. A woman. She happened to come in when the guy was leaving."

Annie frowned. "Did he get away with any money?"

"A few thousand."

Annie's frown deepened. The cold-blooded killer had traded the life of an innocent woman for chump change. And now the family of the dead woman would suffer a lifetime because of one heartless act.

Jake turned off the television and they went back to the kitchen.

He looked at his watch. "I guess I'd better get going. I have to meet Mrs. Overstone at a coffee shop on the other side of town, and I'd better not be late. She sounded rather anxious on the phone."

Annie pointed with reluctance to a wicker basket on the counter. "There're my car keys. Be careful with it," she said, and she knew he would.

Jake grabbed the keys, checked his cell phone, then slung the bag over his shoulder. He turned to give Annie a quick kiss and then went out the front door.

Annie stood in the doorway and watched him get into the car and drive away. She hoped his task wouldn't take too long. She had really wanted to take the car for a spin.

She went back to the kitchen and poured herself another cup of coffee, then went to the office and buried herself in research.

It wasn't all that bad. At least it was quiet, and she had the house to herself again.

CHAPTER 5

Tuesday, 9:28 a.m.

JAKE ARRIVED AT Crosstown Coffee two minutes early and went inside and glanced around. He knew from experience, this small shop on the edge of town was famous for some of the best coffee around. It was usually packed with coffee lovers, and today was no exception.

He maneuvered his way around a long lineup of customers waiting for service and scanned the seating area with his eyes.

The name of the woman he had an appointment to meet was Merrilla Overstone. She had said she'd be wearing a dark green suit. She signaled him with a short hand wave when he spied her over in the far corner, huddled at a small table, her back to the wall.

He acknowledged her wave with a nod and weaved down the narrow aisle between the occupied seats, approaching her table.

"Merrilla Overstone?"

She nodded and motioned for him to take a seat opposite her. "Please, call me Merrilla," she said.

Jake introduced himself and shook her hand, giving her one of his business cards. She glanced at the card as he settled into a hard chair, brushed aside a container of sugar and artificial sweeteners, and dropped his arms on the tiny round table.

Merrilla Overstone was dressed in a well-fitting, dark olive-green business suit with a white frilly blouse underneath the jacket. Jake estimated the woman to be in her midforties. Her slightly roundish face gave her a youthful look, but the worry lines around her troubled hazel eyes showed she was under some recent strain. She sat straight-backed, a small handbag in her lap and a hint of a smile on her lips.

"Thank you for coming," she said in a low voice. Her friendly smile grew wider and she pushed a paper cup toward him. "I thought you might like a cup of coffee. I didn't know how you take it."

Jake popped the top off and took a sip of the hot liquid. "It's perfect," he said. "Thank you."

She cleared her throat and glanced at a couple enjoying a donut for breakfast at a table barely an arm's length away. They paid no attention, and she brought her gaze back toward Jake and leaned closer, speaking in a hushed tone. "As I told you on the phone, I'm sure my husband's having an affair."

"And you want me to get some evidence of his infidelity," Jake said matter-of-factly, keeping his voice low to match hers.

She nodded. "I need real proof." She sipped at her coffee, holding the cup in two hands, pleading with her eyes as she watched him over top.

Jake took a deep breath and sat back. "Here's the thing," he said. "I can surveil him and document where he goes and who he meets. I can take all the pictures you want, but I don't break into houses or pop into bedrooms with a camera in my hand and catch them in the act."

Merrilla gave a weak smile and set her cup down. "I don't need those kind of pictures. If you're willing to help me, I only need to know it's true, and who the woman is, to be satisfied my suspicions are correct."

Jake wasn't curious about what she planned to do with the information he would obtain. These situations often led to divorce, but more often than not, after being confronted with their indiscretions, the guilty party would "fess up" and make an attempt to reconcile. At least, for a while. Often, when things were smooth sailing again, they would slip back into their old habits. Jake had caught more than one repeat cheater.

But he'd keep that to himself unless she asked. He wasn't in the marriage counseling business.

Merrilla continued, seemingly eager to share the details of her suspicions. "My husband's a real estate agent, and since he's on the road a lot, it's hard to be sure where he might be at any given moment."

Jake could see himself running around the city, chasing a man from house to house in the hopes of catching him in the wrong place at the right time. It sounded like a massive and boring chore.

Merrilla allayed his thoughts of an unpleasant and drawn-out job. "He's doing it in our home," Merrilla said. "You only need to watch the house, wait for them, and get some photos of them coming and going. I suspect they meet up there every day, or almost every day."

"Every day?" Jake asked, an unintended note of disbelief in his voice. He noticed Merrilla Overstone was a reasonably good-looking woman, and he wondered what kind of man would have an ongoing affair to such an active degree.

She nodded. "No matter how careful he thinks he might be, I can tell when someone has been there. It's the little things. The smell of strange perfume, the way the towels in the bathroom are folded, and his attempt to remake the bed. And there's more." She sighed deeply, her shoulders slumping. "It's been going on for some time, and a woman always knows."

"Do you have any children?" Jake asked.

She shook her head and offered a weak smile. "We never had time for kids. We both work." She sighed. "Even if I wanted children, it's too late for me now." Her eyes took on a faraway look. "And maybe too late for us, anyway."

Jake took a long gulp of coffee and set it back down, massaging the edge of the cup with his forefinger. He had half a mind to turn the job down. Sometimes he'd rather be out chasing serial killers and mass murderers than sit in the front seat of a car all day.

He looked back at Merrilla and studied her face. The

unhappy look in the eyes of the heartbroken woman was enough to sway him.

"I'll need a retainer," he said reluctantly.

Merrilla smiled with relief, then snapped open her handbag, removed an envelope, and slid it across the table. "There's two thousand dollars in there, as we discussed on the phone."

Jake opened the flap of the envelope and flipped through the bills with a thumb, then slipped the package into the inner pocket of his jacket. "That'll do for a couple of days," he said.

"Let me know if you need more."

Jake nodded. "We'll see how it goes. Did you bring me a picture of your husband?"

She rifled through her handbag, produced a four-by-six photo, and held it out. "Here's a fairly recent shot," she said. "He still looks the same. His name is Niles. Niles Overstone. And he'll be driving a Lexus."

Jake took the photo and glanced at the close-up of a man's face. He looked pleasant enough, with short-cropped hair and warm brown eyes. The man was a couple of years older than his wife, and rather handsome—not in a rugged square-jawed way, but with boyish good looks—and he sported a cheerful smile on his friendly face. But then, you couldn't tell a cheater by looking at his face.

Jake tucked the photo into his pocket alongside the packet of bills. "What about the woman?" he asked. "Do you have any idea who she might be?"

Merrilla shook her head. "I have no idea. Originally, I had the thought of setting up some hidden cameras in the house.

But then I realized that might not work so well. I had no way of knowing when it would be safe to set them up, and besides, I was afraid he might discover them."

Jake nodded and figured she should've gone with her first idea.

"Where does your husband work?" he asked.

"Richmond Realty. It's downtown, but like I said, he's not there most of the time." She produced a business card from her handbag. "Here's his card, and his cell phone number's on there." She frowned. "It might not be a good idea to call him."

"I don't expect I'll be calling him. Maybe his office. I haven't worked it all out yet." Jake drained his coffee and pushed the cup to one side. "I'll probably watch the house until they show up. So, I'll need your address."

Merrilla told Jake her house address, and he wrote it down on the back of Nile's business card along with her cell phone number.

She pointed to the number. "You can call me anytime. Please, keep me informed."

"I will," Jake said, tucking the card into his pocket.

Merrilla looked at her watch and then back at Jake. "If there's nothing more you need, I'm already late for work, and I'd better get a move on."

"I have everything I need for now," Jake said.

"Thank you," Merrilla said with a smile, then she clutched her handbag in one hand and rose to her feet. "I look forward to hearing from you." She wound her way past the waiting customers and out the front door.

Jake swooped up the empty cups and dropped them into the recycle container, then headed out to the car. He called Annie and told her he was taking the job, and that he loved her, and he would see her later in the afternoon.

CHAPTER 6

Tuesday, 10:03 a.m.

JAKE TOOK ANOTHER look at the back of the business card as he turned down Mulberry Lane. According to the information Merrilla had given him, she and her husband Niles lived at number 166.

The houses on Mulberry were of the larger cookie-cutter variety. The subdivision was twenty or so years old—plenty of time to allow each of the similar two-story houses in this mature upper-middle-class neighborhood to develop its own character. Most had a double-width driveway in front of a two-car garage, along with a generous front lawn. Many of the properties were separated from their neighbors by rows of hedges, large shrubs, or blooming flowerbeds.

Jake kept one eye on the house numbers as he eased down the block. Halfway down, he spied the number he was straining to see. He drove past 166, pulled a U-turn, and parked across the street in front of the neighbor's house.

From where he sat under the shade of a maple tree, he had a direct view of the entrance to the Overstone house and the empty driveway in front.

He called Richmond Realty, and a woman with a sultry voice answered the phone. She informed him Niles Overstone was not in his office, but he could be reached on his cell phone or voicemail. Jake said he'd call back later in the day. He decided if Niles didn't show up at the house within the next couple of hours, he would make an anonymous call to the man under some pretense or another.

He thanked her and hung up, turning his attention back to the house. As he stared at the empty driveway, he thought it strange a man would carry on an affair in his own home. Perhaps he felt safe in the knowledge his wife was at work. He never expected to get caught, anyway, and it was because of his own carelessness he was now under suspicion.

Jake unzipped the sports bag that lay on the passenger seat and pulled out the pair of binoculars and the camera. He laid the camera on the seat beside him and scanned the front of the house with the glasses. There was no visible movement through the limited view he had of the front window.

Setting the binoculars down, he took the camera and got out of the car, crossed the street, and walked toward the front of the house. He glanced around and then strode boldly up the driveway and around to the side of the garage.

Pushing open a wooden gate, he went down a stone pathway between the garage and a high cedar hedge bordering the property. He peeked in the small window of an entrance door and frowned.

A bright red Lexus sat in the nearest bay. The other one was empty.

Niles Overstone was home.

Was Jake already too late? Was the girl in there with him, or would she be coming later, if indeed they had a rendezvous planned for that morning?

Jake snapped a few pictures of the inside of the garage, then strode back down the driveway, crossed over the street, and got into the Toyota. He laid the camera on the seat beside him and picked up the binoculars. He'd have to wait until they left.

Annie had insisted on tinted windows in her new car, making it harder than normal to see through binoculars or take photos through the glass. He wound down the driver-side window, stuck his elbow out, and trained the glasses on the house.

Though a handful of cars had eased up the quiet street, so far he hadn't seen any pedestrians. Among the area's residents, like the Overstones, both partners likely worked to maintain their lifestyle in this neighborhood. If they had any children at all, they would be at school or perhaps grown up and moved on.

He settled in, stretched, and yawned. It wasn't necessarily the stakeout itself he didn't like; it was the waiting. Sure, he got paid for sitting in a car doing nothing, but it was boring beyond belief. It was all part of the job, though. He moved the seat all the way back, propped his sunglasses on his nose, then slouched down and waited.

Ten minutes of inaction later, he bolted upright, pulled off his sunglasses, and squinted through the binoculars. A man had been strolling up the street from the opposite direction. Jake hadn't paid him more than a casual glance, but as the man turned and went up the pathway toward the house, he'd caught Jake's attention.

He grabbed the camera and snapped a dozen photos as the man climbed the steps, opened the front door, and disappeared inside.

Jake wondered if the man was Niles, who'd gone up the street for some reason and was now returning. But the sloppy clothes and ragged baseball cap the newcomer was wearing didn't look like the casual dress of a real estate agent. He had zoomed the lens in, but he hadn't been able to get much of a glimpse of the man's face.

Jake squinted at the small monitor and looked through the pictures, one at a time, zooming in on the head of the man. Even though the subject was wearing a baseball cap, making it hard to be sure, the man in the picture appeared to have short hair. Jake decided it wasn't Niles.

The strange thing was that even though Niles was inside, he'd left the door unlocked. There seemed no doubt he was expecting a visitor.

And if Niles hadn't intended to stay long, why'd he bothered to park his car in the garage?

Something was definitely fishy about this whole thing, and it sure didn't look like there was any kind of an affair going on. At least, not a love affair or a sexual liaison. Unless Niles was bisexual. That was a distinct possibility, although Merrilla hadn't so much as hinted in that direction.

Merrilla might be able to identify the man once Jake had a chance to show her the photos. When one or both men left the house, Jake hoped he could get some clearer shots of the visitor.

Perhaps everything was on the up and up, but Merrilla had paid him to do exactly what he was doing. And if everything turned out innocently enough, he'd be happy for the distraught woman.

He reached into the sports bag and removed a carefully wrapped package. The ham sandwiches Annie had put together for him would be a pleasant break. He devoured two of the four, polished off a bottle of water, and decided to save the rest of the food for later.

Five minutes later, he sprang to a sitting position and listened intently. Unless his ears had fooled him, and he was sure they hadn't, he'd heard the distinct sound of a gunshot.

And it had come from inside the Overstone residence.

CHAPTER 7

Tuesday, 10:46 a.m.

JAKE TOSSED THE binoculars onto the passenger seat and jumped from the vehicle. Something unusual and no doubt lethal was going on inside the Overstones' house.

Judging by the dubious appearance of the bedraggled visitor who'd entered the dwelling a few minutes ago, Jake assumed Niles Overstone was in mortal danger. He'd only heard one shot coming from the house, but one was all it took, and Niles might be dead or dying at this very moment.

He dashed across the street at an angle, leaped over a hedge, and crossed the lawn, approaching the large picture window in the front of the house. The curtains were drawn halfway, the balance of the window covered by sheers, and he couldn't make out much of anything inside. He leaned closer, squinting through a narrow gap, and gazed around the living room. It was empty. Whatever had happened, it didn't appear to have taken place in that room.

With three long-legged leaps, Jake reached the front porch and tested the door. It was unlocked. He eased it open and listened, then pushed it open all the way and stepped into a small foyer.

The living room was directly to his left, and a glance confirmed no one was in the room. To his right was a small door. He poked at it with his forefinger and it swung open. It was a bathroom, and it was empty.

The kitchen stood at the end of a short hallway, dead ahead. He could make out some cupboards on the far wall and, from where he stood, nothing appeared amiss.

To his right and slightly ahead, a set of stairs led upwards, no doubt to the bedrooms.

Then a soft groan came from the direction of the kitchen. He crept down the hallway toward the room, being cautious not to make a sound. His running shoe made a soft squeak on the hardwood floor and he froze. If someone had been shot, and the shooter was still in the house, he didn't want to be the next victim.

The problem he faced was whoever had fired the shot might be getting away, and the gunman would be long gone before the first cruiser could arrive. But he had no choice. He had to notify the police before investigating further, and he hoped the pictures he'd snapped earlier would be enough to identify the fugitive.

He reached for his cell phone in the holster at his waist and came up empty. It was in the car. He hesitated a moment, then turned to leave. Another groan from the direction of the kitchen spurred him on, and he turned back and crept forward silently, one careful step after another, as the low groaning continued.

He neared the kitchen, hugging the wall, and peered around the doorway. On the far wall, a door led outside, and it was ajar. The shooter had most likely run out the back way. However, there was a possibility he might still be in the house somewhere, maybe even on the other side of the kitchen, and Jake wasn't taking any chances.

He heard a gasp for breath, and he took a step forward, crossed the hallway, and peered into the kitchen. He stopped short in the doorway, and his eyes popped at the sight in front of him.

The gunman's victim lay flat, blood pooling on the floor, streams of red filling the cracks between the ceramic tiles.

It was Merrilla Overstone.

Jake's mouth hung open a moment, and he stared at the woman, a million questions running through his mind.

What was she doing here? The last time he'd seen her was at the coffee shop, and the woman had said she was heading for work. And where was her husband? Perhaps he was in the garage at this very moment, making his getaway. But if that were the case, Jake would've heard the car start and the garage door open.

Something was amiss, and it didn't make sense.

The woman wheezed and fought for air, jarring him out of his thoughts. She looked at him and attempted to speak, a gurgling sound coming from her throat as she forced out one word.

"Why?"

Her voice was barely intelligible, and she gasped for another breath.

Jake dashed forward and crouched beside the woman, pulling back a flap of her jacket. Her snow-white blouse was stained red, the crimson patch continuing to grow. As far as Jake could tell, she'd been shot at close range, the bullet entering her body somewhere in the vicinity of her heart.

And the shooter had dropped the gun in the woman's lap, leaving the weapon behind before making his getaway.

But Merrilla was still alive, and as long as she was, Jake had to do whatever he could to keep her that way. He was no expert at gunshot wounds, and he had no idea whether or not the bullet had exited her body on the other side. All he could do was stop or slow down the bleeding as much as possible.

He ran to the cupboard and pulled open two or three drawers before he managed to find a towel, then he knelt beside the victim, folded the towel, and pressed it to the wound.

"Hold it there. Hold it tight," he said, looking into Merrilla's fading eyes. "Can you understand me? I have to call 9-1-1."

She gave a weak nod and moved her trembling left hand upwards, placing it over the towel. He put his hand on hers and pressed down. "Hold it as tight as you can," he said, then, satisfied she was, he glanced around the kitchen for a landline. He didn't see one, and he turned back to the victim. "I'll be right back."

He stood, anxious to get his cell phone. As he turned to leave, he glanced down with dismay as Merrilla fumbled for the weapon and wrapped her hand around it. She raised it toward Jake, and her hand trembled as she struggled to put her finger on the trigger.

"Why?" she managed to say, her voice but a whisper. "Why?"

The woman had mistaken Jake for the man who'd shot her, and now she was about to shoot him in retaliation.

He ducked to one side, then crouched down and brushed her hand aside, grabbing her by the wrist. She clung to the weapon, her hand shaking, and he tried to ease it from her weakening grip. As she struggled to retain her hold, the gun fired, the shot almost deafening him as a bullet whistled over her head and burrowed itself in the wall somewhere in the next room.

Then her grasp weakened, and he managed to peel her fingers back and retrieve the weapon.

The back door slammed.

Jake's head shot up, and he sprang to his feet, racing across the kitchen. He whipped the door open and leaped out onto the back deck.

He looked around frantically, but the gunman was nowhere to be seen. Whoever had slammed the door couldn't have gotten away that fast, and Jake decided the breeze blowing through the house from the open front door had created a wind tunnel, causing the back door to close. Nothing else made any sense. If the shooter had been hidden in the kitchen and ran outside, the last thing he'd do was close the door behind him.

Jake glanced around again, scrutinizing the area in case his theory was wrong. His gaze came to rest on a woman's bulging eyes. She was on the adjoining property, crouched behind a low hedge fifteen feet away. Only the top of her head and her startled eyes could be seen.

He stood unmoving and stared back a moment, unable to think straight, not sure what to say or do. Jake assumed the neighbor had heard the shot and come to investigate. He hoped she'd called the police already. He wanted to get back to Mrs. Overstone. She couldn't afford to lose much more blood.

Then the woman's eyes dropped down, and her open mouth opened further as she inhaled sharply and stared at the pistol in Jake's hand.

He looked down at the weapon, then back at the woman, and took a careful step forward. He stopped when she let out a weak, gasping scream.

"It's not what you think," he called. "It's not my gun. Please, call 9-1-1. Mrs. Overstone has been shot."

The woman blinked rapidly a few times, then scrambled to her feet and scurried away. Jake heard the rear door of her house close. He shook his head and went back inside, set the weapon on the kitchen table, and crouched down beside the victim.

He gazed into her pain-filled eyes. "The ambulance is on its way," he said. "You're going to be all right."

Merrilla Overstone fought for air. Her eyes drooped, quivered a moment, then they closed and she lay still. Jake felt her pulse. It was weak, and her breathing was shallow, but she was still alive.

"You're going to be okay," he repeated, praying he was right.

CHAPTER 8

Tuesday, 10:58 a.m.

HANK WAS AT HIS DESK in the precinct when he got notice there had been a shooting. The victim had survived and had been rushed to the hospital. First responders had secured the area, and he was expected at the scene.

The last thing Hank needed was another case. He was neck-deep in his investigation of the bank robbery and the subsequent murder, and it looked like he'd be putting in a lot of overtime for the foreseeable future. As head of RHPD's small robbery-homicide unit, the responsibility was his.

He spun his chair around. Detective King was at his desk, and he appeared to be doing some work for a change. Hank went to King's desk and glanced over the cop's shoulder, surprised to see the detective was studying Buck's statement taken at the bank robbery.

"We have a shooting," Hank said, waving a sheet of paper. "An attempted murder. CSI's already working the scene."

King closed the folder and tossed it onto the desk, then straightened his back and looked at Hank. "We'll take your car."

The two detectives left the precinct and made their way to the parking lot at the rear of the building.

"The shooting's at 166 Mulberry Lane," Hank said as he climbed into his Chevy. "Apparently, there's a witness. A neighbor. She didn't know the victim's name, but she believed her to be the homeowner."

"Mulberry Lane," King said. "That's in a ritzy part of town."

Hank shrugged and turned the vehicle onto the street. "Not that ritzy. More than I can afford, though." He glanced at King. "And more than you ever will."

"I have no desire to live in that part of town, and I don't think a whole lot of the people who do."

Hank smiled inside. Mulberry Lane wasn't far from where Amelia lived, but he wasn't about to tell his partner that.

A few minutes later, Hank eased down a side street and pulled in behind a line of police cars. There was no question as to where the shooting had taken place. Halfway down the block, an entire lot had been secured by crime scene tape. A pair of officers chatted on the front lawn. Another cop was leaning against the wall by the front door of the house.

The CSI van was parked into the driveway, its side door hanging open.

Hank and King ducked under the tape, made their way to the front door, and donned shoe covers before entering the foyer. Hank stopped short when a familiar voice greeted him from the living room. "Hey, Hank. What brings you here?"

Hank turned and did a double take. Jake stood in the middle of the living room floor, a grin on his face, tight-fitting white coveralls covering him from ankles to neck.

"What're you doing here?" Hank asked, a cross between a smile and a frown on his confused face. "And what's that getup you're wearing?"

Jake shrugged. "CSI took my clothes."

Hank's expression didn't change. "Whatever for?"

"They have to check them for GSR, and this jumpsuit was all they had for me."

Hank was more confused than ever, and it was several minutes and several pointed questions later before Hank understood the situation Jake had gotten himself into. But the thing that continued to confuse him was the revelation that the victim's name was Merrilla Overstone.

Hank turned to King. "If you recall, Merrilla Overstone is a loan manager at Commerce Bank. I interviewed her after the robbery. She's the one who ducked down behind her desk."

It was Jake's turn to be confused, and he glared back and forth between Hank and King, a perpetual frown on his brow.

King crossed his arms and scowled at Jake. "What's this all about? Do you know something about the robbery you're not telling us?"

Jake's frown deepened and he stared at King in disgust. "I have no idea what's going on. I was hired to do a job, and I'm as mystified as you are."

"Don't go anywhere, Jake," Hank said. "I'm gonna need your complete statement." He turned to King. "Let's take a look around and see if we can figure out what went on here."

"I got some pictures of the killer entering the house," Jake said. "My camera's in the car."

Hank turned back and looked at Jake in surprise. "I'm gonna need those."

Hank followed King to the kitchen, sidestepped an evidence cone marking a pool of blood in the middle of the floor, and approached Rod Jameson.

"They tested Jake's clothes for GSR," Rod said, his deep voice filling the room. "The results are positive. And his prints are on the gun."

"According to Jake's story, that's exactly what we'd find," Hank said. "Is the witness around?"

"She's waiting with an officer in the backyard," Jameson said, handing Hank an evidence bag. "You might want to see this first."

Hank took the bag and held it up. It contained a cell phone.

"That's Merrilla Overstone's cell phone," Jameson said. "Found it in the side pocket of her jacket. There's a text message you might want to see. Don't worry about prints. It's already been processed." Jameson glanced at his clipboard and turned his attention to another matter.

Hank opened the bag, found the text messages, and read the most recent one. It was from 10:10 that morning, and it read: "Am on my way. Bringing money."

The message was from an unknown sender and there was no reply.

King looked over Hank's shoulder at the message. "What money?"

Hank narrowed his eyes. "Money from the bank robbery, perhaps. This is too much of a coincidence to be otherwise."

"Do you think Mrs. Overstone was in on the robbery?" King asked, leaning against the counter.

Hank frowned. "Maybe. But it seems more likely the robber was afraid she'd recognized him and he had to silence her. We know she saw his face, though it was from a distance away."

"Then where does the money come in?"

Hank shook his head. "I don't know. Perhaps he threatened her and she demanded money. Then the whole thing turned to blackmail."

"And he wasn't too happy with that," King said. "Decided he'd rather shoot her than pay up."

Hank nodded. "Perhaps, but why would he bother confronting her in the first place? Why not shoot her and be done with it?"

"I think she was in on the robbery," King said. "It's the only thing that makes sense. He was bringing her cut to her, then changed his mind about paying."

"You might be right. Let's hope we get a chance to talk to her."

Jameson had returned. "Hank, the witness says she has to go out."

Hank nodded and handed King the phone. "See if you can find out what number that message came from."

He went out the back door. A woman was carrying on a

conversation with a cop, and she stopped speaking when Hank approached her. She introduced herself as Penny Ford and glanced around nervously as though expecting the gunman to return and shoot her down.

Hank jotted her name and phone number down, then asked, "Mrs. Ford, did you witness the shooting, or only hear the shots?"

She glanced around again, then looked Hank in the eye. "I was in my backyard like I always am this time of day." Her jowls quivered when she talked, and she seemed to be chewing her words before she spit them out. "I was minding my own business, and I heard a shot. I ducked down mighty quick, then a couple of minutes later, I heard another shot, and a man ran from the house."

"Did you see where the man ran to?" Hank asked.

"He didn't run nowhere. He just stood still, waved the gun at me, then went back in the house."

The woman was describing Jake's actions. But what about the shooter? "You only saw one man?"

The woman nodded. "Just one."

"After the second shot. And no one ran from the house after the first shot?"

The woman shook her head adamantly. "Nope. Just the one. Not two seconds after the second shot, he comes chargin' out wavin' a gun."

"Could you identify him?"

"Sure as shootin'. He was tall. Taller than you. And big, like strong."

That was Jake, all right.

"Did he say anything to you?" Hank asked.

"He said to call 9-1-1. So I did."

Hank nodded. That's what Jake had told him.

"An officer will take your statement, Mrs. Ford. Thank you for your time."

She grunted and Hank went back into the kitchen. King was still working at the phone. "Did you get the number?" Hank asked.

King nodded, held the phone up, and Hank transcribed the number to his notepad.

Hank's phone rang and he answered it. It was an officer who'd taken up a post at the hospital, guarding the victim in case the shooter attempted to finish the job.

"Mrs. Overstone wanted to talk," the cop said. "I told her to wait for a detective, but she wouldn't. She looked in pretty bad shape, like she could die at any minute, so I wrote it down."

"What did she say?" Hank asked.

The cop spoke in a slow voice as he gave Hank the message. "Merrilla Overstone said it was Jake Lincoln who tried to kill her."

Hank glared at the phone in confusion. It didn't make sense. Jake couldn't be a killer. But it all fit. The woman herself had IDed him as the shooter. And the witness had said there was only one man who had come out the back door, directly after the second shot. Jake Lincoln. And he had gunshot residue on his clothes as well as on his hands, and his prints were on the weapon.

Did that mean he'd also robbed the bank the evening before?

King's mouth was hanging open, and he stared into Hank's eyes in disbelief.

Hank spoke in a hoarse voice. "It's impossible. There's no way Jake had anything to do with this. He gave us a perfectly logical story that explains everything."

"I hate to say it, Hank, but it's just a story. I believe Jake, but the evidence says otherwise." King paused and scratched his head before continuing. "With this kind of evidence, the captain would have our tails and maybe our badges if we didn't bring him in."

Hank blew out a long breath and looked at the floor. King was right. They really had no choice.

King continued, "The evidence points overwhelmingly to a charge of first-degree murder."

Hank nodded, unable to believe the words he found himself saying. "It looks like we have to arrest Jake."

CHAPTER 9

JAKE STRODE DOWN the pathway leading from the front door of the Overstone residence. He ducked under the tape and crossed the street to the Toyota.

He couldn't remember if he'd locked the vehicle or not, but Jameson had been kind enough to give him the key from the stash of his stuff they were holding along with his clothes. It turned out he'd left it unlocked in his haste to investigate the shooting. He got in, set the key on the dash, and picked up the camera, laying it in his lap. Hank would need the photos to help ID the shooter. The camera hadn't caught a view of the man's face, but it would be better than nothing.

He picked up his phone from the passenger seat and dialed Annie's cell number. He hadn't had a chance to call her earlier, and she'd be wondering what he was up to.

She listened with dismay, interjecting a "wow" or a gasp here and there as he explained the unusual situation he was in. "I have to give Hank the camera, then fill out a statement, and I'll come home," he said. "And I have a lot of questions for Merrilla Overstone once she's able to talk to me."

He hung up and searched for a pocket in his jumpsuit. There didn't seem to be any. He put his phone in the glove compartment, picked up the camera and the car key, and stepped out. He stopped short, his hand on the open door, and glanced across the street.

Hank and King were coming down the pathway toward him. The two detectives were flanked by a pair of uniformed officers, their eyes on Jake.

Was Hank in such a hurry to see the pictures on the camera he couldn't wait a couple of minutes? And why was he bringing a pair of cops with him?

As they drew closer, Jake frowned at the somber look on Hank's face. One of the uniforms moved his hand to his weapon, and King looked like he was about to draw, as well.

The truth hit Jake and hit him hard. They were going to arrest him.

He froze, unable to move a muscle as he realized what he was up against. His head spun, confusing questions speeding through his mind. Why would they arrest him unless they thought he was somehow involved in the shooting? Perhaps it was on the strength of the neighbor's testimony. She'd seen him run from the house with the gun in his hand. And Merrilla Overstone had somehow confused him with the real shooter, as well.

But he'd given Hank his story, and as unlikely as the situation seemed, surely his friend had believed him.

The cops were closer now.

Maybe Hank hadn't believed him.

If he was arrested and held, he'd be in deep trouble. Besides Annie, whom could he depend on to figure this whole thing out? Surely the photos he'd taken would exonerate him. But they might not be enough, and if no one believed his story, it could be a very long time before the real truth was revealed. Too long for him to wait and rot in jail.

Now ten feet away, the uniformed cop tightened his hand on his weapon as if ready to draw.

Jake's mind whirled. He couldn't see himself held with the rest of the common criminals. Not that he was afraid, but how would he ever figure this out from behind bars? It would be impossible, and he'd only be able to depend on Annie and Hank. But Annie would be limited, and Hank had to follow the evidence wherever it led, and right now it was leading in the wrong direction.

There was only one choice to make.

Jake dove back into the car, hit the starter button, then pulled it into gear and rammed the gas pedal to the floor. The vehicle sprang ahead, and he was glad they'd bought a car with a lot of pep. But would it be enough?

He glanced in his mirror. One officer was chasing the vehicle on foot, while the other now had his weapon drawn. Hank stood stock still, his arms folded, and King seemed to be reaching for his handgun. Jake assumed they wouldn't shoot at him. Certainly Hank wouldn't, but he had to get as far away as possible.

Was he doing the right thing? Of course, the right thing

was not to run—according to the law. But he wasn't a criminal. He hesitated and let up on the gas pedal. Perhaps he should go back. Running from the law was never the proper reaction—unless you were guilty.

But he wasn't, and he had to prove it.

He touched the brake and spun the steering wheel, turning onto a side street leading off Mulberry Lane. A siren sounded somewhere behind him, and he glanced in the rearview mirror. Flashing red and blue lights were closing in, and he stepped on the gas, gradually widening the gap between him and the law.

Jake took a left-hand turn at the next street. This was nuts. What had he gotten himself into? He thought again about pulling over and getting out. He'd drop obediently to the pavement, facedown, and put his hands behind his back and wait for the inevitable handcuffs. Then they would lead him away, lock him up, and bring the law down on his head.

No. He couldn't let that happen.

Someone had set him up, and whoever was involved had done a good job of framing him. But why had they chosen him? Was he a convenient pawn in the wrong place at the right time? It seemed likely Merrilla Overstone was supposed to have died on the spot and had no idea what was going on, either.

But then, why had she returned home when she'd said she was going directly to work? Had she forgotten something and dropped by the house on the way? But if so, how had the would-be killer known where she'd be? Or perhaps he hadn't expected to see her there, and she'd surprised him, and he'd had to deal with her.

Jake wanted to talk to the woman in the worst way, but it seemed out of the question now. He'd never get close. He had to get away, then talk to Annie about the whole mess. She might be able to come up with some much-needed answers. Of course they'd be keeping an eye on his wife as well, but as long as she wasn't under any suspicion, she'd be free to ask questions of people Jake couldn't get to.

And he had a lot of them.

He took another turn, the police not far behind, their siren still blaring. There was only one vehicle chasing him, but it would be more than enough. No doubt they'd already arranged to set up roadblocks in the area. He'd be trapped soon, with nowhere to go.

He had to ditch the vehicle; it wasn't much good to him now. If by chance he happened to outrun the cops, they'd be scouring the city for the car. It would just be a matter of time before it was spotted.

But first, he had to get out of this neighborhood and get to somewhere more populated. Then he'd have time to think through the situation and come up with a plan.

Jake held the pedal to the floor and the Toyota zipped past a line of parked cars. He wasn't all that used to the vehicle yet, but he clung to the steering wheel, leaning forward as the engine hummed. At least he was in familiar territory now, and he knew Main Street wasn't far off.

He took another left turn and peered through the windshield. The stoplight at Main was red. He couldn't afford to stop for traffic, and he prayed the light would turn green before he reached the intersection.

It didn't.

He looked left and right, touched the brake lightly, and hoped he had judged it right. A truck rumbled through the intersection at Main, Jake's vehicle nearing clipping its tail as the Toyota sped through the red light. The driver of another vehicle coming from the opposite direction laid on his horn and squealed to a stop in time.

He had made it through the intersection safely, but it'd been a close call. Now all he had to do was ditch the cops, then ditch the Toyota. He'd have to go on foot. Otherwise they'd catch him eventually.

He looked in his rearview mirror. The police cruiser had slowed at the light, and it was now easing through the intersection, not far behind him.

Jake took a right turn, pulled to the curb behind an SUV, and jumped from the vehicle.

He was on his own now, wearing a pair of coveralls that would be recognizable anywhere, with no place to run and nowhere to hide.

He was a wanted fugitive, running not from justice, but from injustice.

CHAPTER 10

Tuesday, 12:05 p.m.

HANK PULLED HIS Chevy in behind Annie's Toyota, and he and King climbed out. Although he'd arranged for roadblocks in the area, he wasn't surprised to hear the officers had found the abandoned car. Jake was much too smart to keep driving it around.

What bothered him most was that Jake had vanished. Given the overwhelming evidence, Hank knew he was duty-bound to bring Jake in, but he was finding it hard to believe his friend was a criminal. He'd known him and Annie a long time.

There had to be another explanation.

Hank went to the passenger side of the Toyota and opened the front door. A camera lay on the seat beside a pair of binoculars. Jake had said he'd taken pictures of the mysterious visitor to the Overstone home, and Hank was anxious to see them.

He pulled on a pair of surgical gloves and handed another pair to King. Picking up the camera, he turned it on and fumbled his way through the controls. He raised his head a few moments later, a deep frown on his brow.

There were no pictures on the camera.

Not even one.

Why had Jake lied about that?

"Found a burner phone here," King said, ducking out of the back door of the vehicle. "It was under the seat." He handed the phone to Hank.

Hank took the cell and swiped through it. He consulted his notepad and said, "This is the phone that sent the text message to Mrs. Overstone. It's the same number." He swiped a couple more times and held the phone up for King to see. "There's the message."

"Am on my way. Bringing money," King read.

Why would Jake have been bringing her money? If he'd been doing a surveillance job for her, like he'd said, he wouldn't have been taking her any money. And if he'd gone to Mrs. Overstone's house with the purpose of killing her, he would've had no reason to bring her cash.

Hank pulled out his cell phone and called a number.

"Jameson, it's Hank," he said into the phone when a deep voice answered. "I need to know the contents of Jake's pockets."

"Hold on a sec," Jameson said, then returned a moment later. "There's a business card here. Richmond Realty. It's Niles Overstone's card. The house address and a phone number's on the back." He read out the number.

Hank glanced at his notepad. "That's Mrs. Overstone's cell number," he said. "What else?"

"There's an envelope here stuffed with bills." The sound of rustling paper came over the line, then Jameson continued, "All fifties. Do you want me to count it?"

"Yup."

A few moments later, Jameson said, "Two thousand in fifties."

"Anything else? No cell phone?"

"His wallet, his watch, a few loose coins, a photo of Niles Overstone, and a ring of keys. That's everything."

"Thanks, Jameson," Hank said and hung up. He scratched his head. The take from the bank robbery was forty-eight hundred. Two thousand was less than half, but if Merrilla Overstone had been blackmailing Jake and demanding a cut, that might've been the agreed-on amount.

According to the bank manager, each bill in the stack of hundreds stolen during the robbery was marked. The fifties weren't marked, so there seemed to be no way of tracing the envelope full of cash back to the robbery. He made a note in his pad to check with the manager again, but it seemed doubtful she'd be able to identify the cash.

Hank wondered why Jake would have a business card from Richmond Realty, and he was anxious to talk to Niles Overstone. Had Mr. Overstone hired Jake to kill his wife? If so, where did the bank robbery fit in?

Or perhaps Mrs. Overstone had recognized Jake at the robbery, told her husband, and the two had concocted a scheme to blackmail Jake. All the evidence appeared to fit that scenario. If so, Niles Overstone's life might be in danger. Did Jake have a photo of Niles Overstone with him so he'd know what the man looked like when he came for him?

And the thought that Annie might've known about this whole arrangement disturbed Hank deeply.

Annie was a close friend of his, and he'd need to have a long talk with her. And unfortunately, he'd have to obtain a search warrant for the Lincoln residence. The thought of digging through the private affairs of his friends nauseated him, but he shook it off and forced himself to concentrate on the task at hand.

Hank ducked back into the front seat of the car and opened the glove compartment. An iPhone sat on top of a stack of papers. He turned it on and a picture of Annie appeared. It was Jake's cell phone.

He checked the recent calls, squinting at the last inbound number. Jake had received a phone call from Merrilla Overstone at 9:03 that morning. That had to be when he'd arranged to meet her.

Hank leaned back in the seat and closed his eyes. The evidence against Jake was mounting. Rather than coming up with something that would exonerate his friend, all he'd found was more damning evidence.

He wondered if it was really true. Was the friend he'd known for so many years nothing but a thief and a murderer? The thought was ridiculous.

The trunk slammed and Hank opened his eyes as King approached the side of the vehicle. "Nothing in the trunk, Hank," he said. "Just a spare tire."

Hank nodded. "Nothing else in the back?"

King reached into the backseat and removed a sports bag. "A couple of sandwiches and some water in here."

"Anything else?"

"Nope."

Hank sighed and stepped from the vehicle. "All right. Let's get this car towed in." He took a deep breath and let it out slowly. "Then we'll organize a manhunt and find Jake."

King crossed his arms and frowned at Hank. "This is hard on you, isn't it, Hank?"

Hank nodded. He wasn't sure if he was angry with his friend, or disappointed. Maybe both. And perhaps heartbroken about the whole thing. Whatever it was, he had a job to do, and friend or not, he had to bring Jake in.

King glanced around, then spoke again. "I find it hard to believe, too, Hank. If there's another answer, we'll find it."

Although King didn't seem deeply affected personally by the ongoing revelations, at least he appeared to have a heart somewhere under that tough skin of his.

Hank glanced over as the Channel 7 Action News van pulled up behind his car. Somehow Lisa Krunk had managed to track him down, and he had no chance of escape this time. He had to stay here until Annie's car was towed into the police impound lot.

He watched in disgust as Lisa climbed from the passenger seat. Her driver and cameraman, Don, opened the rear door and removed his camera, dropping it on his shoulder.

Hank'd had a lot of run-ins with Lisa in the past, some good, mostly bad, and he knew the pushy newswoman would do anything for a story. Her brand of sensational journalism was well known throughout the precinct, and she was never content until she could spin a story to her liking.

Lisa's extra-wide mouth was twisted into a smile as she approached the cops. She wore an unbecoming floppy red hat, her short dark hair barely reaching her ears.

"Good afternoon, Hank," she said, looking down her long thin nose at him, her microphone stuck in his face. "Can you tell me anything about what happened on Mulberry Lane?"

Hank strove to remain patient and glanced at the red light on the camera, then spoke into the mike. "There was a shooting at the residence, and it's an ongoing investigation."

"Do you have a suspect?" Lisa asked.

Hank hesitated. "The assailant had left the scene before we arrived. We're looking at a number of people, but I can't tell you more than that."

Lisa glanced at the Toyota. "Is this the suspect's vehicle?"

Annie and Lisa were well acquainted—not friends, but they'd had occasion to meet many times in the past. Had this been Annie's old Escort, Lisa would likely have recognized it. But Hank didn't want to mention Jake and Annie's names. At least, not yet.

"This vehicle might or might not have been involved. We don't know for sure," he said.

Lisa persisted. "Can you give me the name of the victim?"

"Not until the family has been notified," Hank said. He paused and then added, "I don't have anything else for you. There'll be an official statement later when we know more."

Lisa swung the mike toward King and opened her mouth

to speak. King shrugged and walked away. Lisa frowned and turned back to Hank, the frown replaced with a fresh smile. "Thank you, Hank," she said and turned to Don. She dragged a finger across her throat and the red light went out.

Hank's jaw dropped as Lisa and Don walked away. She was usually more persistent and much more obnoxious than this. Was she losing her edge? Hank hoped so, but he doubted it.

He figured she'd be snooping around again as soon as she thought up a new angle.

Hank closed the doors of the Toyota and leaned against the hood. As soon as the tow truck got here, he could leave, and he was determined do all he could to get to the bottom of this whole mess.

CHAPTER 11

Tuesday, 1:12 p.m.

ANNIE DROPPED HER book on the stand beside her easy chair and went to answer the ringing doorbell. She was surprised to see Hank standing on the porch, a somber look on his face.

A sad smile touched the detective's lips. "Can I come in? I need to talk to you."

"Of course," Annie said. She waved him into the foyer and led him to the living room, settling back into her chair as Hank dropped onto the couch.

He observed her, tapping his fingers nervously against his leg, his uneasy eyes on hers. Then he breathed a short sigh and cleared his throat. "Have you talked to Jake recently?"

Annie narrowed her eyes. "He called me two or three hours ago and explained the situation. It's a little unusual, but I haven't heard from him since." She paused and her frown deepened. "Is something the matter?"

Hank raised his eyes and stared blankly at something behind her as if gathering his thoughts. When he looked back at her, his deep brown eyes seemed to penetrate her soul.

"As you know, Annie, we've been friends a long time," he said. "The three of us. And that's why this pains me so much." He paused again, his eyes never wavering, then spoke slowly. "There's overwhelming evidence Jake was involved in a shooting."

Annie tilted her head to one side. "A shooting?"

Hank nodded. "It appears he had an appointment to meet a woman, and he was bringing some money to her that might be connected to the bank robbery."

"Impossible," Annie said, a hint of annoyance in her voice.

Hank shrugged. "There's more. The woman was shot, and we aren't sure if she'll survive. There seems to be no doubt Jake fired the weapon. A neighbor claimed to have heard two shots, the last one immediately before Jake ran from the house with a pistol in his hand."

Annie sat back. "How can you possibly assume it was him who fired the gun?"

"Jake had gunshot residue on his clothes. And of course, his prints were on the gun."

"That's not enough," Annie said, her frown of disbelief deepening.

Hank's voice quivered when he spoke. "The woman, Mrs. Overstone, said it was Jake who shot her."

Annie stared at Hank, unsure what to say. This was preposterous. Jake would never shoot an innocent person.

"Did you talk to Jake about all this?" she asked.

Hank nodded. "I talked to him briefly before we did any further investigation. Before all the evidence against him came to light."

"And?"

A look of pain appeared in Hank's eyes. "Jake lied to me, Annie." He cleared his throat again. "He claimed he was staking out the house and took photos of someone entering the premises." Hank shook his head. "He never took any photos."

Annie looked around as if half-expecting Jake to appear and tell them what had really gone on. "Where's Jake now?" she asked.

"I don't know."

Annie gave Hank a blank stare.

"He ran. He was in the car, and we came out to, uh … talk to him, and he took off." Hank dropped his head a moment, twiddling his fingers. Then he looked back at Annie. "The truth is, Annie, I had no choice but to arrest Jake, and he knew it. So he ran. He got away in the car and then abandoned it after a few blocks."

"Did you try to call him?"

"He left his cell in the car."

"But surely you don't think Jake's guilty of anything," Annie said. "Especially murder."

"There's a lot more evidence than what I've told you about, and there's nothing that supports his story." Hank sat forward. "Further evidence points to Jake's involvement in the bank robbery."

"Now you've gone too far," Annie said in a sharp voice. "Jake was on a stakeout when it happened. You were here when he came home."

Hank spoke in a soft voice, probably in response to Annie's growing anger. "If we can confirm that, it'll go a long way toward proving Jake's innocence."

"He told you where he was. He was following around a woman whose husband suspected she was having an affair."

Hank sighed. "That's the problem with those kind of jobs. He has to remain unseen or it's not effective. Unless somebody can testify he was doing what he said he was …"

Annie leaned forward. "You have the video from the robbery. Surely it'll prove Jake had no involvement."

"The video isn't clear, Annie. And no one had a good view of the robber's face."

Annie sat back, crossed her arms, and lifted her chin. "What's Jake's motive for doing any of this?"

Hank hesitated. "The woman who he … who was shot … is a loan manager at the bank that was robbed. Though she said she couldn't identify the robber, we know she saw his face from a distance. We think he felt the need to eliminate her to be safe."

"If that's the case," Annie said, "how would the bank robber know who she was? If she couldn't recognize him, how could he recognize her?"

"I don't know. Perhaps he was familiar with the bank."

She knew Jake was very familiar with the bank and many of its employees, but she kept the knowledge to herself. If this didn't get straightened up soon, that information would come out eventually. But right now, Annie had no intention of adding more circumstantial evidence to the already growing list against her husband.

Annie dropped her hands to her lap and stared at the uneasy cop. "What's your opinion about this?" she asked flatly.

Hank took a deep breath. "I honestly don't know, Annie. It ludicrous to think I've known Jake all these years and never really knew him. I'm a cop. It's my job to know people. I find the whole situation hard to swallow, but the evidence …"

Annie glared at the cop in disappointment. He didn't sound too convinced of Jake's innocence.

Hank reached into his pocket, removed a folded piece of paper, and unfolded it thoughtfully. He leaned forward, hesitated, then handed it to Annie.

"I want you to know how much this pains me," he said as she took the paper. "But we have to search your house."

Annie's eyes widened as she stared at the search warrant. Then she looked into Hank's troubled eyes. They seemed to be almost begging her to forgive him for the necessary intrusion.

She swallowed hard, handed the warrant back to Hank, and nodded in understanding. "Okay," she said in a hoarse voice, her anger dissipating.

Hank was only doing his job, and besides, they had nothing to hide.

"We'll be careful," Hank said as he stood. He gave Annie one last look of apology, then went outside.

Soon the front door opened, and Hank came back in,

followed by Detective King and a pair of investigators. Annie sat silently in the living room as her house was searched and her privacy was invaded, her heart silently breaking for her husband.

A few minutes later, Hank came back into the living room and dropped onto the couch. He carried an evidence bag containing a white envelope.

He held up the bag, the sadness in his eyes replaced by a look of deep pain. "I really shouldn't be showing you this, Annie," he said. "But since we're friends, I have to tell you what Detective King found in the garage."

Annie stared at the bag.

"It's money. Twenty-eight hundred dollars." He paused, then continued, "It was found in Jake's tool chest. If you add it to the two thousand Jake was carrying, it's the exact amount taken at the bank robbery."

Annie's mouth dropped open, and her wide eyes stared at the impossible evidence.

Hank continued, "The hundreds taken at the robbery are marked, and the serial numbers were recorded. We'll have to check these against the list to be sure, but on the surface, it doesn't look good."

Now Annie had to make a decision—either to believe in her husband's innocence, or to accept the overwhelming evidence against him as the truth.

The latter was inconceivable, the former the only choice to make.

"He's innocent," Annie said in a firm voice. "You'll see."

Hank stood and went to the door. "I hope you're right,"

he said, glancing back at her. "I sure hope you're right."

She looked meekly at the cop. "Can I have my car back?"

Hank's shoulders slumped and he turned to face her. "It ... it's evidence," he said, then sighed deeply and opened the door. "I'll see what I can do."

She watched Hank and the other three cops get in their vehicles and drive away.

And now, it was up to her. She had to find Jake. Or wait until he found her. Then, together, they could get this ridiculous situation straightened out.

CHAPTER 12

Tuesday, 2:35 p.m.

JAKE HAD SPENT THE last two or three hours making his way through the city, taking side streets and alleys as much as possible, working his way north. He was sure the police would have a BOLO out on him by now, and the snow-white jumpsuit he wore would be a dead giveaway to any cop on the prowl.

When he hit Front Street, he wondered why he hadn't thought of the idea sooner. It was a warm day, so he went into a small neighborhood park and ducked behind a group of bushes, obscured from the eyes of any passersby. He stripped off his jumpsuit, then tugged and pulled, managing to rip off the top half of the suit. When he put it back on and rolled up the pant legs, he figured no one would look at him twice. His outfit looked a little odd, but he could pass for just another jogger out for some afternoon exercise.

He had to get somewhere safe and think this whole thing

through. He'd been framed for attempted murder, possibly even murder, and with his best friend against him, there were very few people he could turn to.

First, he needed some clothes and some form of transportation. Just about anything would be suitable—a bicycle, a motorcycle, or a car.

He had no money and no phone. He had to live on the streets, at least for the time being, but he knew exactly where to go.

Homeless by choice for reasons he hadn't cared to share, his friend Sammy Fisher was the obvious guy to turn to. Sammy knew the streets inside and out, sharing a kinship with those who called cardboard boxes and alleyways their homes. The quaint but lovable man had been helpful to Lincoln Investigations in the past, and at the very least, Sammy would help him get something to wear.

Jake continued along Front Street, turning his head away whenever he met a pedestrian or when a vehicle breezed by. He was in the open now, and he was ready to run should a cop happen to drive by and get the notion to stop and question him.

A few minutes later, he neared the Richmond River overpass. He hopped a low barrier and faced a steep embankment. A hundred feet below, the river flowed south toward Lake Ontario. It was a pleasant spot, and it was Sammy's backyard.

Jake eased down twenty feet, ducked under the overpass, and smiled when he saw the place where Sammy had carved out his niche. Directly under the overhead street, up where the bank touched the underside of the concrete and steel overpass, what Sammy called his "castle" was hidden from anyone who might chance to wander nearby.

The homeless man had dug out a ten-by-ten cave, boarded up the walls with whatever he could find, and covered the front with a soil-stained canvas. It was invisible to all except those who knew of its existence. Insulated from the wind and the weather, it could be heated by a candle in the winter, and was cooled in the summer by the earth surrounding it.

Jake pulled back the canvas and peered inside. A pot or two hung from the ceiling, a thick blanket lay on a bed of cardboard, and the rest of Sammy's meager possessions occupied a small shelf unit. But Sammy wasn't there.

Without a watch, Jake was hampered, but the sun told him it was nearing midafternoon. He knew Sammy did his scrounging in the morning, enjoyed whatever he could find for lunch in a park somewhere nearby, then returned to his castle for a quick afternoon nap. He should be along anytime.

Jake dropped the canvas flap back into place and climbed down the bank to the river. He sat down on a rock and waited.

He had to come up with a plan. One thing was obvious—if Hank had intentions to arrest him, then there must be more evidence than Jake knew about. What else had Hank found at the crime scene that would force him to take such extreme measures?

Perhaps the neighbor. There was no doubt she'd seen him, and he had been carrying the pistol at the time. He'd have gunshot residue on his clothes. But he'd explained all that to Hank.

As he contemplated the events of that morning, playing them back in his mind, a sudden realization hit him. Merrilla Overstone had been delirious with pain when he'd found her, and she'd mistaken him for the shooter. If she'd told the police the same thing, along with the rest of the evidence, her allegation would be severely damaging to his story.

He stood, brushing his thoughts aside as a man moved toward him from a hundred feet away.

It was Sammy, no doubt.

A scruffy man approached, a wide grin splitting his heavily bearded face. He stopped, pulled off his faded baseball cap, and ran a hand through his mop of dark hair.

"It's good to see you, Detective Jake," Sammy said, plopping his cap back on and squinting through one eye. "What brings you to my humble abode?"

Jake shook his hand. "I need your help, Sammy."

"Have a chair," Sammy said, pointing to the rock.

Jake sat back down. Sammy kicked off his ragged running shoes and sat on the grass. He leaned back, supporting himself with his arms, and looked at Jake through intelligent blue eyes.

"I'm in a jam," Jake said. He told Sammy some of the details of his predicament. "I have no money, I can't go home, and I need some clothes before I can work this out."

"Boy, you sure got yourself in a mix-up. I'll be overjoyed to do whatever I can," Sammy said. "But what about Detective Annie? Can't she do something?"

Jake shrugged. "I have no phone, and I haven't been able to talk to her since this morning. I have no idea what's going on with her."

The tip of Sammy's beard poked against his once-white t-shirt as he talked. "Clothes are no problem, Jake. The folks at Samaritan Street Mission take good care of us when we can't take care of ourselves. Food, clothes, even a warm bed in the winter." He gave Jake the once-over and grinned. "I can pop over there and see if they have any extra-extra-large stuff that'll fit you."

"That'd be great, Sammy. I'd go myself, but they know me there, and I have to keep a low profile."

"No problem. And I bet Mrs. Pew will lend me a bike from the mission's thrift shop. They usually have one or two in decent condition." He tugged at his beard a moment. "Can't help you with a cell phone, though. And I got no money. I could always panhandle for an hour or two and scrounge you up a few dollars if you'd like."

"That would be great, but forget the money," Jake said. "Just the clothes and a bike are good. And I'll make it up to you, Sammy."

"No, you won't. I know for a fact you and Annie give money to the mission every month, and what you do for them, you do for me and others less fortunate than me." He gave Jake a mock scowl. "So you won't mention that again."

Jake grinned. "Duly noted."

"Then let me get on my way, and I'll be back quicker than a jackrabbit."

"There's one more thing, Sammy."

"Sure."

"The guy who shot Mrs. Overstone looked to me like a good-for-nothing hood. Probably known among some of the seedier elements of the city." Jake paused and shrugged. "You helped me dig up the hiding place of a jailbird before. I thought maybe you might be able to help again this time."

"We'll talk about that when I get back," Sammy said. "I got people everywhere. Some smart, some not so smart, but if I have something to go on and ask enough questions, we might be able to track him down."

"I really appreciate this, Sammy."

"Well, it's not just for you. It's for me and mine as well. Anytime you rid the streets of lowlife scumbags, it makes it safer for all of us." Sammy stood. "Just relax and don't worry. I got your back." He turned and strode up the riverbank.

Jake watched until his friend disappeared from view. Hank knew Sammy from a past case, and he hoped the cop wouldn't think of looking him up.

But he knew Hank had a job to do; finding Jake was his duty. Given their friendship, he prayed Hank would be a little less eager to do that task in a timely manner, allowing Jake some freedom to track down the real criminal.

As soon as Sammy came back, he had to find a way to contact Annie. He had no doubt his wife would be under scrutiny from the police, and he didn't want to compromise her freedom in any way.

That was the last thing either one of them could afford to have happen.

CHAPTER 13

Tuesday, 3:12 p.m.

HANK POPPED THE LID off the container of physical evidence gathered at the scene of the shooting of Merrilla Overstone. He sat at his desk and tipped the box toward him, studying the articles it contained.

Along with Jake's personal effects and Merrilla's cell phone, the items of most interest to him were the pistol and the bullet it had fired. He took the bag containing the weapon from the box and turned it over in his hands.

The gun was a .22-caliber semiautomatic Beretta, one of their cheaper models, but readily available on the streets at double or triple its retail value. If you had enough money and the desire to acquire them, weapons of all kinds could easily be obtained on the black market.

Hank pulled a file folder toward him and browsed through the information obtained from the hospital via an earlier phone call. Preliminary data indicated Mrs. Overstone had suffered a penetrating chest wound, and the bullet had lodged in her chest wall. According to word Hank had gotten, surgery to remove the bullet had been successful, and though the victim had suffered severe trauma, she'd been given a good chance of survival.

Hank reached into the box and removed an evidence bag containing the bullet extracted from the victim. He hadn't been surprised when the ballistics report had confirmed the weapon used to kill the woman at the bank was the same one used to shoot Merrilla Overstone.

Though they were separate incidents, the shooting of Mrs. Overstone and the bank robbery were not only related, they were bound together by a single item—a weapon.

If Jake had indeed robbed the Commerce Bank, there was no doubt he was also responsible for the attempted murder of Mrs. Overstone.

Hank was struggling to come up with a motive. The shooting of Merrilla Overstone was a direct consequence of the bank robbery, that much seemed certain, but what'd been Jake's motive for robbing the bank?

Jake wasn't stupid. Surely he knew there wouldn't be much money had by robbing a bank, and he had enough knowledge of law enforcement never to attempt such a foolhardy scheme. And he and Annie certainly didn't need the small amount of money that'd been taken.

And yet, the stack of hundred-dollar bills had been found in a tool chest in Jake's garage. The serial numbers had been compared to the bank's records, and they matched.

Everything pointed toward Jake being the perpetrator of both crimes, and thus far, there was nothing to confirm his story and prove his innocence.

The only indication Jake's account might be true was the presence of Merrilla Overstone's fingerprints on the envelope of money. Hank quickly dismissed it as convincing proof. Jake could've handed the envelope to Merrilla before he'd shot her, then taken it back. Certainly that's what the prosecutor would argue in court.

He looked up as Detective King approached his desk and sat on the edge of the guest chair.

"I've confirmed Niles Overstone's at the Richmond Hill General Hospital," King said. "He went there as soon as he heard about his wife, and he hasn't left since. He's expecting us."

Hank laid the weapon and bullet back in the evidence box, put the lid on, and stood. "Let's go, then." He picked up his briefcase and turned to King. "I'm very interested in what Mr. Overstone has to say."

When they reached the hospital, they made their way through the silent halls and took the elevator to the third floor. They found Niles Overstone alone in a small waiting room not far from the intensive care unit. The man looked beaten down, lines of worry etched on his brow.

Overstone tossed a magazine aside and stood as they approached. He gave the cops a forced smile and shook their hand when Hank introduced them, then dropped wearily back into his chair.

Hank took a seat in a plush chair across from the

distraught man and leaned forward, setting his briefcase on the floor beside him. King occupied an adjacent chair and slouched back, his arms resting on the comfortable armrests.

Hank began, "Mr. Overstone, I'm very sorry to hear about your wife."

Overstone nodded in recognition, then narrowed his eyes and asked, "Have you found out who did this yet?"

"Not yet. We have some leads, and we're doing everything we can to find the perpetrator."

"You have a suspect?"

Hank hesitated. "We have a possible suspect."

"Has he confessed?"

"Not yet. We're still trying to find him."

Overstone frowned.

"We'll get him," King put in.

Hank silenced King with a look. He didn't like to make promises like that. He could only assure victims they would do whatever they possibly could.

King shrugged and tapped his fingers silently on the armrest, gazing around the small room.

Hank pulled out his cell phone, then stood and crouched beside Overstone's chair. He swiped the screen a couple of times and said, "I'm going to show you some photos. Tell me if you recognize anyone."

It was Hank's mobile version of a police lineup, and most of the photos were of cops. Hank had found it useful in the past to help confirm the identity of someone by adding the person's picture to the standard group of images.

Overstone agreed and looked at the cell phone, squinting

at each photo as Hank swiped through them. He pointed to the last one, a glint appearing in his tired eyes. "I recognize him."

It was a photo of Jake.

"How do you know him?" Hank asked.

"I've seen him on the news. It's Jake Lincoln. Just two or three days ago, Merrilla and I saw a news story about him and his wife."

Hank watched Overstone's reaction. "Do you know him from anywhere else?"

Overstone looked at the photo again and shook his head. "Should I?" He paused and then asked with a frown, "Is he involved with the shooting of my wife?"

Hank moved back to his chair and sat down. "We think he might know something."

Overstone appeared bewildered as he looked back and forth between Hank and King. "Haven't you talked to him?"

Hank hesitated and King spoke. "He claims he was hired by your wife. According to him, your wife said you were having an affair."

Overstone's frown deepened. "That's preposterous."

"Are you having an affair, Mr. Overstone?" King asked.

"Absolutely not."

"Was your wife having an affair?"

Overstone shook his head firmly. "Never," he said in a raised voice. He glanced around, then lowered his voice and continued, "It's ludicrous to suggest either one of us was."

"We have to ask," Hank said. "This is all for the record." He paused before continuing. "I'm sorry, Mr. Overstone, but

I also have to ask where you were this morning between ten and eleven."

Overstone sighed and rolled his eyes. "I was showing a house," he said, remaining patient. "I don't have the phone numbers of the prospective buyers with me, but you can check with my office. They'll give you the number and you can call them. They'll confirm it."

"We will," Hank said. "Thank you."

Overstone dropped his elbows on the armrest and rested his chin on a tightened fist. "Wouldn't it be better to find out who did this rather than making ridiculous accusations?"

"They're only questions, sir," King said. "Not accusations."

Overstone glared at King, his nostrils flaring. "They sound like accusations to me. Next you'll be accusing me of shooting my own wife."

"Did you?"

Niles bolted to his feet and stared down at King. "I think we're done here."

King looked up at the angry man. "Mr. Overstone," he said calmly, "Jake Lincoln had your business card with him. Did you give it to him?"

"He could've picked it up at the office. I have no idea how he got it."

King continued, "He had written your wife's name and phone number on the back."

Overstone crossed his arms. "You'll have to ask him about that."

The angry man stepped back as King rose to his feet and said, "I will. Thank you for your time."

Hank stood and offered his hand. Overstone refused the gesture and continued to glare at the cops.

Hank turned to leave, following King from the room. He didn't like making pointed accusations, but he had watched the man during his verbal exchange with King, and Hank was convinced Overstone was telling the truth.

"The man's under a lot of stress," Hank said to his partner when they were out of Overstone's earshot. "Did you really have to be so hard on him?"

"He'll get over it," King said with a chuckle. "Soon as we find out what's going on and make an arrest, we'll be his best buddies." King looked at Hank. "Besides, I'm not sure the man's totally innocent. I think he knows something."

"Look, King," Hank said. "If he hired Jake to shoot his wife, why would he identify him in the photo?"

King shrugged. "Who knows? Maybe to cover himself. Felt he had to identify him. A lot of people know the Lincolns. Jake's involved in this, and if it came out Overstone was lying about knowing Jake, who knows what else he's lying about?"

Hank sighed and shook his head. "King, that doesn't even make any sense."

"Makes sense to me," King said. He touched Hank's arm and came to a stop.

Hank turned to face King and waited for the cop to continue.

"What if the Overstones cooked up some scheme together to rob the bank, and they hired Jake to do it?"

Hank couldn't help but laugh. "That's the dumbest theory I've ever heard."

King chuckled and continued down the hallway. "Yeah, I guess it is kinda dumb."

But other than the obvious, Hank had no theories that made any sense, either. He had to give his partner credit for trying.

CHAPTER 14

Tuesday, 4:24 p.m.

JAKE PACED BACK AND forth by the edge of the river, anxious to get out of there and do whatever he could to find out who'd set him up. But he had to wait for Sammy to return.

He spun around and glanced up the embankment toward the sound of a ringing bell. It was the old-fashioned kind from a bicycle, and Jake grinned to see Sammy easing a bike down the steep grade toward him.

Jake's grin turned to a frown as Sammy approached, still ringing the bell and chuckling.

"It's all I could get," Sammy said, coming to a stop beside Jake. "Sorry about the color."

"It's a girl's bike."

Sammy shrugged. "It's not really pink. More of a burnt purple."

"It's pink, Sammy."

"I think that's the least of your worries. Hey, if people are looking at your bike, they won't be looking at you."

Jake laughed. "It'll do. Thanks, Sammy."

"And that's not all," Sammy said. He pushed down the kickstand and reached into his pocket. He pulled out a small bundle of bills and handed it to Jake. "Told you Mrs. Pew was amazing. She lent me a hundred bucks, no questions asked."

"How'd you manage that?" Jake asked, taking the bills and thumbing through the twenties.

"I put in the odd day there. Just helping out. Been doing it for a long time." He pointed a stern finger at Jake. "But you gotta pay her back when this is all over."

"With interest," Jake said.

"And there's more," Sammy said, popping up the lid of a yellow basket attached to the rear of the bike. He pulled out a plastic bag. "Here's your duds. They should fit."

"I hope they're not girls' clothes."

"How'd you know?" Sammy said, finger-combing his bushy beard. "What better way for a man to hide than by wearing a dress?"

Jake frowned and opened the bag, then grinned and pulled out an extra-large pair of faded blue jeans and a black t-shirt, complete with a belt and baseball cap. He held up the pants. "They look like a perfect fit."

Sammy cocked a thumb over his shoulder. "You can change in my castle."

"I'm not that modest," Jake said, kicking off his shoes. He stripped off what was left of the jumpsuit, tossed it aside, and pulled on the jeans. He tightened up the belt, donned the loose-fitting t-shirt, and put his shoes back on.

"You look great," Sammy said. "You're better dressed than me, now." He reached back into the basket and removed a package. "It's a burner phone," Sammy said, handing the bag to Jake. "Thought you might wanna call your wife." He pointed to the phone. "I got Mrs. Pew to activate it for me. She had to do it online."

"You've thought of everything, Sammy. I don't know what to say."

Sammy shrugged. "Don't say anything. Just catch the guy who set you up."

"I'm gonna need your help with it, but I don't have much to tell you. All I know is someone tried to kill Merrilla Overstone, and it wasn't me."

Sammy pushed up his cap and scratched his head. "That doesn't give me a lot to work with."

"Give me a minute," Jake said. He fiddled with the phone a moment and then dialed Annie's cell number.

"It's me," he said when Annie answered.

Annie breathed out a long sigh of relief. "Am I glad to hear from you. I had no idea what's going on."

"I'm okay," Jake said. "I'm at Sammy's. He set me up with some clothes, a bicycle, and a burner phone."

"Hank was here," Annie said, then paused before continuing. "They searched the house."

"I have nothing to hide."

"Jake, listen to me," Annie said. "Whoever set you up did a thorough job. Someone planted money in the garage and

King found it. Hank thinks it's from the bank robbery."

"The bank robbery?" Jake said in confusion. "What does that have to do with all this?"

"It's all tied together somehow. Merrilla Overstone works at the bank that was robbed."

Jake's mouth dropped open. Now it was starting to make some sense. Merrilla Overstone worked at the bank and might've seen the robber's face. The thief had tried to kill her to cover himself. "And they think I robbed the bank," Jake said in a flat voice.

"That's where the evidence points."

"Was there no video?"

"The robber wore a mask most of the time. The brief shot of his face isn't clear enough to ID him."

"And now I'm wanted for murder as well," Jake said.

"Yes," Annie said. "But I can read Hank. Though he's doing whatever he can to find you, I can tell his heart's not in it."

"Do you think I should turn myself in?" Jake asked, not convinced it was a good idea.

"I'd like to think truth will win out in the end," Annie said. "But I'm not so sure. There's more."

"More?"

"Hank said there were no photos on the camera. He thinks you lied to him."

This was getting worse and worse all the time. Had Jake been the victim of a carefully arranged plan? Or was it possible Merrilla Overstone had told the shooter the house was being watched, and then he'd used Jake as a convenient scapegoat?

Jake knew there were pictures on the camera; he remembered swiping through them. Who could've erased them? It had to have been the guy who came into the house. Or were there others involved?

"Jake, the worst part is Mrs. Overstone said it was you who shot her," Annie continued.

"She was delusional when I found her," Jake said, then hesitated before asking, "I hope you don't believe any of this?"

"Not a word," Annie said.

"How is she? Did the ambulance get there in time?"

"Last I heard, she was fine."

That was good news. Though she'd IDed Jake as the shooter, she might see things differently if she survived. His fate appeared to be in the hands of others.

"We have to meet," Jake said.

"I don't have a vehicle. The police impounded it, and the garage is sealed off. They won't let me take the Firebird. Give me your number, and I'll call you when I can get access to some transportation."

Jake gave Annie the number and then hung up. He had to think this through.

Sammy stood with his hands in his pockets, his usual happy face now grim. "Bad news?" he asked.

Jake nodded. He filled Sammy in on what Annie had told him. "Now we know what we're looking for. If you can get any information on who robbed the Commerce Bank or planted the money in my garage, it'll help a lot."

Sammy cocked his head. "Any idea what the guy looks like?"

"Nope. I didn't see his face. But he was fairly large and muscular, and he was wearing sloppy clothes and a ragged baseball cap. And he had short hair."

"I'll ask around," Sammy said. "And I'll get everyone I know on it. These kinds of people like to talk. They brag to their buddies about what they've done." He shrugged. "I'm betting somebody knows something."

"Just get me a name," Jake said. "One name. That's all I need."

"I'll get right on it," Sammy said, waving toward his castle. "You're welcome to stay here tonight. I could always use the company."

"I'll let you know," Jake said.

Sammy turned away and strode up the bank. "You know where I live," he called over his shoulder. "Check back with me tonight or tomorrow morning, and I'll let you know if I found out anything useful."

Jake watched his homeless friend disappear in the distance, then sat on the rock and considered his current situation. And there didn't seem like much he could do at the moment.

He really wanted to talk to Merrilla Overstone, but he'd never get close to her. Niles Overstone would be the next best thing, but there was no doubt he'd be at the hospital, and Jake would have no safe access to him, either.

Until he had a lead to follow, Annie would have to be his eyes and ears. If Hank was as uncertain about Jake's guilt as Annie supposed he was, then the cop could be counted on to consider the evidence with an open mind.

Hopefully, Hank would keep Annie informed of any developments. If not, she'd find a way to get it out of him.

Jake was looking forward to meeting with his wife. He didn't want to put her in danger or make her appear culpable, but unless Sammy found out something he could run with, Annie was his only hope.

CHAPTER 15

Tuesday, 5:45 p.m.

ANNIE KNEW JAKE was quite capable of taking care of himself in just about any situation, but the circumstances they found themselves in now were way beyond anything they'd ever expected. Jake's freedom was at stake, and the stability of their family was Annie's chief concern.

Matty had no indication anything unusual was going on, and Annie had hoped to keep it that way. But unfortunately, it didn't look like this muddle was going to get sorted out anytime soon. Jake wouldn't be home tonight, and Annie struggled to come up with something she could tell her son.

But right now, she had to arrange to meet Jake somewhere. She needed a vehicle and a babysitter.

Chrissy, Annie's friend from next door, was always willing to watch Matty whenever she was available, and Annie had hoped to borrow her car, as well.

But Chrissy would be out for the evening, so there went the babysitter and the transportation.

That left her with only one option.

Her mother.

Annie bit the bullet and made the call she was dreading. Yes, her mother was quite willing to watch Matty for the evening, and she promised to be there just after eight. Annie had hoped for an earlier time, but her mother was at work, claiming the place would fall apart if she weren't there to keep it together.

Not that her mother needed the job. Annie's father owned a small trucking company, doing mainly local deliveries, and her mother's part-time job at a hair salon only served to fill her otherwise idle days. Annie's father didn't complain, and Annie suspected he was a happier man when his wife was out of the house.

Annie had some time to spare and some things to do. She assumed Jake would be hungry—he just about always was—so she put together a stack of sandwiches and leftover chicken along with some fresh fruit. She'd give him whatever spare cash she could come up with as well, and it would be enough to keep him going for the time being.

She went into the office, spun her chair over to the filing cabinet, and sat down. She leafed through their prior cases, looking for anyone who might be out for revenge and had decided framing Jake for murder was the best way to get back at them.

After several minutes, she gave up. She couldn't find even the remotest connection to the Commerce Bank or to the

Overstones. All of the really bad guys they'd helped track down were either dead or in prison. Unless any of the people involved in their noncriminal cases were nuttier than she thought, it seemed too extreme to suspect any of them would go to such lengths for retaliation.

The question she was faced with wasn't only who, but why. She decided it wasn't revenge. If anyone was so inclined, there were much easier ways to settle a score.

Merrilla Overstone was the key to unraveling the mystery. If Annie could only talk to her ...

Other than the victim, what else did she have to go on?

She pulled open her desk drawer and removed a magnifying glass and a small flashlight. She tested the batteries. There was lots of juice.

Grabbing her keyring from her handbag, she took the items and went out the front door. She went along the front of the house, then up a path to the side of the garage, and crouched down in front of an entrance door crisscrossed with yellow crime scene tape. Flicking on the flashlight, she examined the lock through the magnifying glass.

Though barely discernible, even through the glass, she saw faint scratches around the entrance to the keyhole. And the scratches were fresh. There was no doubt in her mind the lock had been picked, and this door was how the intruder had entered the garage to plant the incriminating evidence.

They rarely used this door, usually accessing the garage through an entranceway leading from the kitchen.

Annie stood and gazed at the door.

All she had proved was the trespasser knew how to pick a

lock. She already knew the money had been planted as part of the frame-up.

Annie tried the door. It was locked. King had entered the garage from the kitchen, so the invader had locked up behind him when he'd left.

Selecting a key from her ring, she unlocked the door, wove her way through the tape, and stepped inside. Sunlight streamed into the dim garage from a rear window and glared off the trunk of the Firebird. She flicked on a light switch and went to the window. It was securely locked, and it didn't look like it had been tampered with.

Jake always kept the garage spotless, and though she studied the floor thoroughly, she didn't see any footprints, and nothing appeared out of place. She pulled open each of the drawers in Jake's tool chest where the money had been found and came up blank.

She left the garage, locking up the door behind her. As she headed around to the front of the house, she stopped short.

Her brand-new Toyota stood in the driveway, and Hank was climbing out from under the steering wheel. A cruiser stood waiting at the curb—Hank's ride back.

"I pulled a couple of strings," the cop said with an unsmiling face as she approached him. "It's the least I could do."

She took the car keys he offered and tucked them into the pocket of her jeans. "I appreciate it, Hank."

The detective cleared his throat and looked down at his shuffling feet. "Annie," he began, looking back up before continuing, "regardless of how I feel about this case, and no matter what the evidence shows, I know you think Jake's innocent."

"Of course."

Hank looked away and seemed to be considering his next words. He took a deep breath and looked at Annie, a slight frown on his face. "Annie, it's my duty to warn you not to harbor Jake. If you have knowledge of his whereabouts and don't tell me, it's a criminal offense."

"I'm aware of the law," Annie said.

Hank paused and appeared to be forcing out the words as he spoke. "Then you're also aware aiding and abetting a murderer makes you culpable."

Annie put her hands on her hips and glared at Hank. "Jake's not a murderer."

Hank shuffled his feet again. "I've done my duty." He sighed deeply. "So, if you know anything, you'd better not tell me."

Annie breathed a small sigh of relief, offering a hint of a smile. "I won't." Her smile widened. "And if you know anything, I won't tell anyone you told me."

The cop shook his head slowly. "I'm afraid I have no good news. Forensics determined the pistol used in the bank robbery was the same one that shot Mrs. Overstone."

"I assumed as much," Annie said and then asked, "How is she?"

"She's not out of the woods yet. She's still in the ICU, and I haven't been able to talk to her. I've left word I need to see her as soon as she's able."

"What about her husband?" Annie asked. "Is it possible he was involved?"

Hank shook his head. "I've checked out his alibi. He was showing a house. That's not to say he doesn't know anything about it, but unless there's something I haven't thought of, I have no reason to think he was involved."

"And yet, you're going on the assumption Jake was?"

"It's more than an assumption, Annie. It's the evidence. And to make matters worse, I can't confirm Jake's alibi. I talked to the man who'd allegedly employed him for that evening, and though it appears to be on the up and up, I can't place Jake anywhere for certain at the time of the bank robbery."

"He wasn't at the bank," Annie said flatly. "And he didn't kill anyone."

"Annie, we found a burner phone under the front seat of your car. There was a text message, sent from that phone to Mrs. Overstone's cell phone."

Annie tilted her head. "And?"

Hank paused. "The message said he was bringing her some money."

Annie frowned. "What does that prove?"

"Nothing for certain. But the supposition is, he was bringing her a cut from the bank robbery. Perhaps blackmail."

"That's absurd," Annie said.

"Perhaps," Hank said thoughtfully. "Perhaps it is."

"It is," Annie said. "And your job is to find the truth. Whether you want to admit it or not, Hank, you know Jake's innocent."

Hank cleared his throat. "I have to get back at it," he said, turning to leave. He stopped and turned back. "It would be best if Jake surrendered. Running makes him look guilty. Although, I really don't expect you'll be seeing him."

Annie thought she saw a twinkle in Hank's eye before he turned away and strode toward the waiting cruiser.

CHAPTER 16

Tuesday, 6:39 p.m.

WHEN HANK GOT BACK to the precinct, he went immediately to Callaway's desk. The young cop was a high-tech genius and, as far as Hank was concerned, an absolute wizard with anything computer related. Callaway was indispensable when it came to ferreting out nuggets of information that might otherwise go undiscovered.

Callaway had repeatedly gone over the video of the bank robbery. Other than a pixelated blowup of the robber's face, he'd been unable to find anything that might help to identify the thief. Hank had viewed the disturbing video many times as well, and now as he leaned in to the monitor, he was still unable to rule out Jake as a viable suspect.

If it wasn't Jake, what could be seen of the bank robber bore an uncanny resemblance to his friend. He had the same muscular appearance, the same towering stature, and even moved in much the same manner. Whether or not it was Jake, the unclear facial features could easily be perceived from a distance as Jake's.

Hank sat back and looked up at Callaway, who was leaning over the desk. "What do you think, Callaway? Is that Jake?"

Callaway blew out a long breath. "I've been over this thing a thousand times, Hank, and I can't give you a positive answer. Physically, he looks like Jake. There's no doubt about that. But when you see how coolly he raises the gun and shoots the woman, well, that ain't Jake."

Hank had watched the cold-blooded killing of the woman—every time he went over the video. And he cringed each time the victim crumpled to the floor just before the killer turned and ran. He hated to think his longtime friend could be so heartless.

But if this case ever went to trial, the video, along with the other evidence, would be more than enough to convince a jury of Jake's guilt.

Hank leaned in a little closer to the screen and squinted as the video replayed the horrific scene near the front door of the bank. He pointed to the monitor. "Was it my imagination, or did I see a reflection in the glass when the security guard pulled the mask off?"

Callaway leaned closer, worked the mouse, and then paused the video. "It's a side view," he said. He took a screenshot and did some fiddling in Photoshop, and the image became clearer.

But not clear enough. The side view of the robber proved nothing either way.

"I think we've squeezed out about all we're gonna get from this video," Callaway said.

Hank sighed and sat back. He had a lot of evidence—all circumstantial—but what he wanted was some cold hard proof. Mrs. Overstone's testimony was the closest thing to that necessary proof, and if it was to be believed, Jake was the killer.

But until Hank was fully convinced, bringing Jake in was a task he approached half-heartedly. Captain Diego had been eyeing him, and Hank assumed the captain was making sure he treated this case like any other.

Diego could rest assured Hank was doing his utmost. A BOLO had been issued, and a search for Jake was underway. Perhaps not convinced of Hank's dedication, Captain Diego had supervised the organizing of the manhunt himself.

Hank had considered asking Diego to excuse him from the case, but he'd dismissed the thought immediately. He'd stick it out as long as Diego allowed. The Lincolns and RHPD had had a close relationship in the past, and Jake and Annie had proven invaluable to his investigations many times. Hank knew Diego had a soft spot for the investigators as well, but the captain didn't have the option of backing away. Especially when it could mean his career if he showed partiality and was wrong.

Callaway interrupted Hank's thoughts by digging through a stack of folders on his desk, pulling one out, and dropping it in front of Hank.

"Here's the info you asked for," the whiz said. "Phone records and financials."

Hank took the folder and stood. "Thanks, Callaway," he said. He went back to his desk, dropped into his chair, and opened the folder.

He looked up as Detective King approached his desk. King settled into the guest chair opposite Hank and sipped at a cup of coffee a moment before speaking.

"Just got back from Richmond Realty," King said. "Overstone wasn't there, but I interviewed everyone in the office." He shrugged. "According to the general consensus, Niles Overstone is the epitome of a gentleman. I was almost laughed out of the place when I questioned one woman regarding the possibility of him having an affair."

Hank waited patiently while King paused and took a big bite of a blueberry muffin, washing it down with a gulp of coffee.

King continued, "They all said pretty much the same thing. The guy talks about his wife more than anything else." King shrugged. "If he's getting some on the side, he's sure fooling a lot of people."

"And Mrs. Overstone?" Hank asked.

"Pretty much the same thing. Though they don't know her all that well, her coworkers at the bank said they never had any indication she could be having a fling. Just not the type, they said. Kind, gentle, and quiet." King took another gulp. "Doesn't prove anything, really, but that's what I got."

Hank nodded. King's findings appeared to confirm what Hank had already suspected. Neither husband nor wife was having an affair.

King stood. "Think I'll get another muffin and then head home. You need anything else?"

"Not tonight," Hank said, then frowned. "We have to get back at it early in the morning, so don't be late coming in."

"No problem," King said, then wandered toward the rear of the precinct.

Hank turned back to his desk and browsed the folder.

Callaway had obtained the complete financial records of the Lincolns, along with the recent phone records of both the Lincolns and the Overstones.

He looked through the Lincolns' financials first. He made some notes and some calculations, then sat back and studied what he had found.

Annie had gotten a new car a couple of days ago. It would take a sizable amount of money to pay for it, but they'd given the dealership a large down payment and financed the balance through the Commerce Bank. That still left them with a healthy business bank account, and their personal savings account had been growing steadily for some time.

Hank didn't see the Lincolns' dealings with the Commerce Bank as a factor. It was a business-friendly bank, and a lot of companies dealt with them. Nonetheless, he wrote himself a reminder to check with the bank manager again to see if she could shed further light on the situation. Although the exact details of the car loan would require a warrant, it didn't seem necessary at this point.

On the surface, the Lincolns' records pointed to one conclusion—there was no need for Jake to rob a bank. If he had, his motive didn't appear to be related to a financial need.

The phone records were next. He was especially interested in the last couple of weeks. A call had been made to Jake from Mrs. Overstone's cell phone. He already knew that. Her phone was in evidence along with Jake's cell and the burner phone. Other than the known calls, Hank couldn't find anything that stood out.

But to be thorough, everyone on the lists would need to be identified and contacted. It would be a time-consuming job, but it was one he'd put Detective King to work on. Rather than spending so much time lounging at the watercooler or half-asleep in the break room, his partner could do some mundane tasks for a change.

Besides, Hank had other things to do. Things that didn't require King's particular style of police work.

He glanced up as an officer approached his desk and handed him an evidence bag. "This is from Jameson," the cop said. "They found the other bullet. Apparently, it was missed at first because it was lodged under the base of a window frame."

Hank took the bag and held it up. According to the written information, the bullet had been found embedded in the far wall of the living room that adjoined the kitchen.

That fit the neighbor's story of hearing two shots. The weapon's capacity was ten rounds plus one in the chamber. The gun had contained eight remaining rounds when it was found. It appeared the killer had started with a fully loaded weapon before the bank robbery and, when all was said and done, had fired three.

CSI had determined the trajectory of the bullet had been at an upward angle, most likely originating from a spot one to two feet above where the body had been found.

That also fit Jake's story. He'd claimed the gun had fired during his struggle to free it from Mrs. Overstone's grasp. But it could also mean whoever had killed her had missed with the first shot, or perhaps with the second.

Hank looked at the bullet, then at the folder of financial information, and wondered what it all proved.

CHAPTER 17

Tuesday, 8:13 p.m.

ANNIE WAS PLEASED TO have her car back for more than one reason. She hadn't been able to take it for a spin yet, but more importantly, she'd been dreading the thought of asking to borrow her mother's car. How could she tell her mother her brand-new vehicle was in the police impound lot? It was going to be hard enough to explain Jake's absence.

She went into the living room and sat on the couch and looked down at her son, who lay on the floor reading a comic book.

"I have to go out for a while, Matty," she said. "Your grandmother will watch you while I'm gone." She glanced out the front window, wishing her mother would hurry it up.

"Have fun," Matty said without looking up. Then he turned his head and looked at his mother, a light frown on his face. "When's dad coming home?"

"Your father won't be home tonight," Annie said, struggling to come up with a story that was mostly true. "He's on a very important job, and it might take him a while."

"Is he undercover?"

"Something like that."

Matty's frown deepened, then, finally satisfied with her answer, he went back to his comic book.

So far, Hank had kept the information about Jake being a fugitive out of the news. Annie was thankful for that, but she also knew it wouldn't be long before someone in the press got wind of the situation. News like that always leaked eventually, and when it did, Matty would be sure to hear about it.

She could explain it away to her son, but her mother was a different story. Annie knew the woman would latch onto the news and use it to justify the negative view she already had of Jake. Annie was having second thoughts about calling her, but she'd had no choice.

When her mother finally pulled into the driveway, Annie went outside to meet her. She waited on the front porch as her mother strode up the pathway, a tight smile on her face.

Alma Roderick was approaching sixty years old and, despite her usual sour disposition, had kept a youthful appearance. Whenever she allowed her tight lips to unfurl into a smile, it could be seen she was still an attractive woman, much like how Annie would look in another thirty years.

After an obligatory air kiss, Alma stood back and frowned

at her daughter, giving her the once-over. "Have you gained a little weight?"

"No, Mother. Not an ounce."

Alma gave Annie another quick look. "So, where're you two off to tonight?"

"It's just me. Jake's out on a job, and he's going to be late. I have to take some stuff to him."

Alma frowned lightly and then nodded as if she understood. Annie was glad her mother didn't wonder why, if she was only making a quick delivery, she couldn't take Matty with her.

"I might be late, and Matty has school tomorrow," Annie added, just in case.

Alma brushed past her daughter and went inside, Annie following behind. No matter how nasty her mother could be at times, she always treated Matty like a prince, and Matty thought the world of his grandmother. That was something, at least.

Annie warned Matty not to stay up late, then grabbed the package she'd prepared for Jake and went out to her car. She called Jake's burner phone and notified him she should be at the overpass in a few minutes.

As she pulled from the driveway, Annie felt a little nervous about breaking the law. She respected the law and the legal process, but this time, the law was flat-out wrong.

She glanced in her rearview mirror as a car pulled from the curb several houses behind her. The gray car looked like just about every other car on the road, and that's what made her suspicious. Unmarked police cars always did. And this one, though keeping its distance, seemed to be following her.

She kept an eye in the mirror as she turned onto Main. In a moment, it was three cars back, and when she took a left at the next street, her suspicions were confirmed when it followed.

Circling around the residential block, she turned back onto Main and headed in her original direction, the unmarked car not far behind.

Annie wondered if Hank was aware she was being watched and followed everywhere she went. Hank was a cop, but he was also a friend. His parting comment to her had indicated that although he knew she'd be having some contact with her husband, he'd overlook it. To deceive her would've been a dirty trick, and she decided Hank wasn't aware of the situation.

Of course, it might not be a cop, but Annie couldn't think of anyone else who might be interested in where she went.

But cop or not, Annie had no choice—she had to ditch the tail.

She smiled. She knew exactly how to do it without drawing suspicion toward herself.

She drove casually along Main for two or three minutes, the car following, then she put on her blinker and took the second entrance into the lot of Main Street Toyota.

It was the large dealership where she'd purchased her new car, and she knew the property was packed, back to front, with brand-new vehicles.

Many exactly the same as hers.

She drove down a wide lane toward the rear of the

building. To her left and right, new cars shone in the late-evening sun. Others cruised the lot, some being bought, still others in for service. All around her, prospective buyers took their sweet time while eager salesmen chomped at their bits.

When Annie reached the rear lot, she glanced in her mirror. The tail had just pulled in. She gave it some gas, spun along the back of the building, then circled around to the third row of cars and stopped. The tail didn't appear to be following. He might be waiting for her at the front.

It took a few minutes, but Annie finally saw what she was waiting for. A vehicle exactly like hers had pulled from the service garage and was heading for the front of the building, down the lane where she'd come in.

Annie waited, then spun down the opposite side of the lot toward the other exit onto Main. She slowed at the corner of the building, then stopped, poking the nose of her car ahead enough to see the tail sitting and waiting, facing the other way, but no doubt keeping a close eye in all directions.

The other white Toyota appeared fifty feet beyond the tail, heading for the far exit and the street. Annie had no doubt that, for a few precious moments, the driver of the unmarked car would be intent on determining whether or not the vehicle was Annie's. She could picture him leaning forward, squinting at the license plate.

Giving her enough time to ease forward and pull onto Main Street, leaving the tail wondering what had happened.

She smiled to herself as she hit the far lane and passed another vehicle. She kept an eye in her mirror, but the persistent gray car never reappeared. Would she see it again, its driver waiting and watching near her home when she got back?

A couple of minutes later, she eased onto Front Street, took the wide road south a couple of miles, then pulled to the side of the road short of the Richmond River overpass.

Jake stepped into view from behind a concrete abutment, a big grin on his face as he approached the vehicle.

"We'd better make this quick," Annie said after Jake had gotten in and welcomed her with a smothering kiss. "This might not be a safe place to stop."

"They'd never catch me anyway," Jake said. "My legs are too long and all they'll see is my back. And they'll never shoot me in the back."

"I would've been here earlier," Annie said. "But I had to ditch a tail."

"A tail?"

"I think it was a cop. Not sure." Annie reached into the backseat, retrieving a stuffed grocery bag. She handed it to Jake. "There's some food in there for you and Sammy along with the other stuff you needed."

Jake opened the bag, peeked inside, and pulled out his extra watch and an iPad mini.

"Thought you could use the iPad," Annie said. "It's fully charged, but use it sparingly."

Jake stuffed the tablet behind his belt and put the watch on. He reached into the bag again, removed a wad of cash, and put it into his side pocket.

"There's five hundred there," Annie said, motioning

toward the money. "That should last you. It might not be safe for us to meet again until this is cleared up."

"Soon, I hope," Jake said.

"I hope so, too," Annie said. "But there've been some new developments."

Jake looked at Annie and frowned.

Annie continued, "Hank told me they found a burner phone in the backseat of this car when they searched it."

"A burner phone?"

Annie nodded. "With a text message to Merrilla Overstone's cell stating you were bringing her some money."

"Not me," Jake said.

"I know it wasn't you. That's just what the text said."

"It was planted at the same time the photos were erased," Jake said, scratching his head.

"There's more," Annie said. "The gun that shot Mrs. Overstone was the same one used in the bank robbery."

"I'm not surprised to hear that," Jake said. "We knew it was related somehow."

"Hank also checked Niles Overstone's alibi. It's solid, but that doesn't prove he wasn't involved in this somehow."

"I'd like to talk to him," Jake said, then asked, "How's Merrilla?"

"Still in intensive care," Annie said, glancing at Jake's attire. "Where'd you get the clothes?"

"Sammy picked them up for me."

"Are you going to stay with him?"

Jake shrugged. "I don't have much choice."

"Tell him I said hello and thanks."

"I will." Jake grinned and gave Annie another kiss. "You'd better go." He opened the door and climbed out.

Annie watched him disappear down the bank, hoping he'd be careful, then she pulled a U-turn and headed for home.

There wasn't much she could do tonight, but bright and early in the morning, she'd figure out a plan of attack.

CHAPTER 18

DAY 3 - Wednesday, 6:45 a.m.

LISA KRUNK ROLLED out of bed, determined to make the day count. She'd been following the story of the bank robbery as well as the Overstone shooting, and she was perturbed that, even with her array of contacts, she'd been unable to find out the names of the suspects.

There wasn't going to be much of a story if no one was talking. The half-dozen short interviews with bank employees were practically useless on their own without some real substance to back them up.

Hank had been tight-lipped about both matters, and though she'd tacked together a couple of short pieces for yesterday's news, they hadn't even been remotely interesting enough to command the top spot.

She was finding it a continual fight to sustain her undeniable reputation as the best TV journalist this town had ever seen—and no doubt ever would.

After a quick breakfast, Lisa took her usual care in selecting the proper wardrobe. Her attire had to be eye-catching, yet professional. Then once her face was fixed to perfection, and her short black hair was stylishly arranged, she admired herself in the full-length mirror and set her mind to the day's tasks.

The evening before, she'd found an indisputable connection between the two shootings. It turned out Merrilla Overstone worked as a loan manager at the bank that was robbed. Lisa's first mission was to follow up on the connection and get to the heart of the story. If the two crimes were indeed connected, then it gave her twice the chance to make something out of it.

The problem was Mrs. Overstone was in the hospital, and though Lisa had employed all of her bountiful charm on the officer on duty outside the ICU, she'd been unable to get to the woman. After finding out Merrilla was incoherent, she decided a couple of camera shots would've been sufficient for the time being.

But that'd been a dead end, too.

And Mr. Overstone had been dodging her calls since this whole thing started. Apparently, he'd been spending most of his time at the hospital, and Lisa hadn't been able to obtain access to the ICU.

When her cell phone rang, she hurried to the kitchen to answer it. The moment the caller identified himself, she knew her persistence was paying off.

It was Niles Overstone, and he wanted to talk.

"I'll be happy to meet you anywhere you choose," Lisa

said. "I need to hear your story and put the vicious rumors to rest."

"What rumors?"

Lisa thought quickly. She had to put him at ease and convince him she was on his side. At least, for the time being.

"Rumors you and your wife are deeply involved in something illegal," she said. "I'll put an end to it with your help."

Overstone sounded confused. "I haven't heard anything about that."

"Where would you like to meet?" Lisa asked.

"I've been spending my nights at Richmond Inn," he said. "It's close by the hospital. My house is still sealed off."

"I know the place. I'll meet you there in half an hour," Lisa said.

Overstone agreed, giving her the room number, and she hung up.

This interview was a step in the right direction. Mr. Overstone was closer to the story than other contacts she'd made, and she was determined to milk him for all the information she could get.

She glanced at her watch. The phone call had put her a couple of minutes behind. She stepped to the window, pulled back the curtain, and peered down seven floors to the circle drive leading into her apartment building. Her faithful cameraman had already arrived, and he was dutifully waiting at the curb below.

Lisa grabbed what she needed and headed downstairs, giving Don a curt hello and quick instructions as she settled into the passenger seat of the Channel 7 Action News van.

Don sped from the lot, and twenty minutes later, the van eased into the driveway leading to the sprawling Richmond Inn.

The Inn, built about fifty years ago, would never be Lisa's first choice in accommodations. Its posted room rates and promise of free breakfast every day seemed attractive until one got a better look around. The almost-vacant parking lot suggested that choosy travelers had bypassed the establishment in search of a more desirable place to spend the night.

Lisa pointed. "Cabin seven. Right there."

Don pulled the van into the parking spot in front of cabin seven and jumped out. He grabbed the camera from the back and hoisted it onto his shoulder. Lisa glanced at a white Lexus parked in front, then made her way to the room door and knocked.

A middle-aged man opened the door, a forced smile on his boyish face. He motioned them in, dropped into the room's only chair, and sat with his hands in his lap.

Lisa glanced at the unmade bed and decided she'd stand.

Don moved to one side where he had a good view of both parties and waited for Lisa's cue.

She signaled him, the red light glowed, and Lisa spoke. "Mr. Overstone, it's come to my attention the bank robbery and the unfortunate attempt on your wife's life might be related. Can you comment?"

"I really have no knowledge of that. It seems feasible, though, and that's what the police are presuming. As much as

I've tried, Detective Corning hasn't told me what the connection is."

"And as yet, the police have no suspect. Is that correct?" Lisa asked.

Overstone hesitated, then said, "The detective showed me some photos to identify. Though he didn't implicitly state any connection, he showed a lot of interest when I identified Jake Lincoln."

"Jake Lincoln?"

Overstone shrugged. "I got the feeling he's involved somehow."

"Perhaps he and his wife are investigating the case?"

"No. It's more than that."

"Have you talked to the Lincolns?"

"No. Never. I'm only aware of who they are."

This was an interesting tidbit. If the Lincolns were in on the investigation, surely they would've contacted Niles Overstone or appeared at the crime scenes. One way or another, Lisa had always managed to run across them during any case they were working on.

Could Niles's assumption be correct? Was Jake suspected to be involved, and that's why Hank had been so close-mouthed? But Lisa had known the Lincolns for some time, and she was finding it hard to believe. They had often risked their own lives to prevent an innocent person from being harmed.

She'd have to dig into this a little further. With a possible name to go on, it would be easier to get at the truth through her connections.

She put her speculation regarding Jake Lincoln on hold and changed the subject. "Tell me about your wife, Mr. Overstone."

Overstone's eyes seemed to cloud over as he glanced at the ceiling a moment before speaking. "My wife's the best thing that ever happened to me." His lips tightened. "The idea she might've been criminally involved with something is absurd. She has no need to be. We live quite comfortably."

"Perhaps she witnessed the bank robbery, and the robber tried to eliminate her," Lisa suggested.

"She never saw his face. She told me that."

"Perhaps the thief didn't know for sure."

Overstone sighed. "We've never told anyone this. Even our friends don't know, but my wife was diagnosed with inoperable pancreatic cancer just over a year ago."

"I'm very sorry to hear that," Lisa said as sincerely as she could manage.

The distraught man nodded in recognition of Lisa's comment before continuing, "She has good days and bad days, and she's finally come to accept the harsh truth. She only has a few months, maybe a few short weeks, left, but on her good days, she's determined to carry on as long as she's able and enjoy what time she has left."

"Why're you telling this now?" Lisa asked.

Overstone looked down at his fidgeting hands, then back at Lisa. "Whoever did this to her has taken away much of the precious time we have left together. I want the world to know what kind of a woman she is." He shrugged and sighed. "Maybe it'll help find out who tried to kill her."

"Are the police not aware of this?"

"I doubt it. She's in intensive care, and no one but myself has any kind of access to see her. I assume the doctors at the hospital are aware of her condition, but perhaps they're keeping her medical history out of this. Or maybe the police aren't asking. It's not really important to the case."

Lisa bit her lip and glared at Overstone down her long sharp nose. In light of the news he'd revealed to her, accusing the Overstones of having affairs or any criminal involvement wouldn't come across in the right way to her countless fans. And since her fans were the most important, she decided to put any accusations on hold for now.

This was turning into a human-interest story and, as always, she had to find a way to bring a little dirt into it without appearing heartless.

Lisa stifled a yawn as Overstone rambled on and on about his wife, Don patiently capturing the lengthy monologue.

When he was finished, Lisa thanked him and stood, forcing her wide mouth to twist into a pleasant smile.

As she and Don left the man behind, Lisa's mind whirled with ideas. By the end of the day, she hoped to have enough to edit together a piece worthy of her adoring fans.

CHAPTER 19

HANK DROPPED HIS briefcase beside his desk, checked with Callaway to see if the whiz had dug up anything new, then wandered into the break room for a cup of sludge. The room was empty, which probably meant King hadn't arrived yet.

After fixing up his coffee as much as possible with some cream and a generous helping of sugar, he sat at the break room table, sipping his drink and considering his next move.

The day before, he'd obtained the information from Annie regarding the supposed stakeout Jake had been on during the time of the bank robbery. The detective had spent much of the prior evening, as well as an hour this morning, doggedly retracing Jake's steps as much as was possible.

If Jake had been following the suspected cheater around, then he'd done a good job of staying invisible. Hank was unable to find anyone who'd seen Jake or the woman he claimed to have been tracking.

Though the absence of information wasn't evidence of Jake's guilt, it also didn't do a thing to prove his innocence. In fact, except for the lack of a motive, there was nothing to show Jake had not been involved in the death of an innocent woman and the attempted murder of another.

Hank had also done a background check on Arlina Madine, thoroughly researching the murder victim at the bank robbery. He'd come up blank. It seemed certain the murdered woman had no connection to the case and was just the unfortunate victim of circumstances.

He set his cup on the table and glanced toward the doorway as a young officer poked his head in, a silly grin on his face and a scrap of paper in one hand. It was Officer Spiegle. The cop usually served at the front desk, a position that fitted him well; he wasn't a whole lot of good for much else. Going by the name of Yappy for no obvious reason, in spite of his shortcomings, he was well liked for his amiable and helpful attitude.

The officer wandered in and sat opposite Hank. "Just got word from the hospital, Hank." He paused and consulted the paper. "Someone by the name of Merrilla Overstone is awake and the doctor said you can talk to her briefly."

Hank jumped up and dumped the rest of his muddy drink down the drain. "Thanks, Yappy," he called over his shoulder as he hurried from the room. He glanced around the precinct floor. Officers and detectives scurried to and fro. Phones rang and were answered. The place was a hub of activity, every cop accounted for and doing what they did best.

Except for Detective King.

Hank shook his head, perturbed at the cop's tardiness, though not surprised. Unless he was on the streets following up a lead or doing an interview, King usually wandered in half an hour late.

He grabbed his briefcase, nodded at Yappy on the way out, and hurried to his car parked at the back of the precinct.

He jumped into his vehicle, brought it to life, and glanced at an approaching car. It was King.

Hank opened his window and waited until his partner had parked his vehicle and stepped out.

King swaggered over to Hank's Chevy and leaned down, looking at Hank through the driver-side window. "What's up?" he asked.

"Mrs. Overstone's awake. Get in."

King scurried around the front of the vehicle and got in the passenger side. He stifled a yawn and fastened his seat belt.

Hank pulled from the lot and turned onto the street. "Can't you be on time for once?"

King shrugged. "I was working late. Besides, nothing much happens in the morning."

"The least you could do is change your clothes once in a while," Hank said, then left it at that when King shrugged again. There wasn't much point in arguing. King would never change.

When they reached Richmond Hill General Hospital, Hank pulled into the circle drive and stopped short of the main entrance, and the two cops got out. The sticker visible on the windshield of his car would prevent an eager officer from having it towed away.

They took the elevator to the third floor and Hank tapped on the opened door of Mrs. Overstone's room. Niles Overstone sat in a chair pulled up close to the bed, holding his wife's hand. When the detectives entered the room, Overstone glanced toward them and then laid his wife's hand gently on the bed and stood to greet them.

A nurse was at the bedside, checking the IV drip, adjusting tubes, and monitoring beeping life support devices. She glanced at the cops as they approached. Her upraised finger along with the expression on her face warned them to be quiet. Hank glanced at King and decided his partner would know enough to behave himself.

Niles Overstone shook Hank's hand and nodded at King, a grim expression on his face. "She's awake, and the doctor says she's stable."

"We just need a few minutes," Hank said. "I only have a couple of questions for her."

Hank glanced at Mrs. Overstone. The woman lay with her eyes closed, her arms resting at her side. An IV drip was taped securely to her pale white skin. The slight up-and-down movement of the sheet gave the only indication the woman was alive and breathing.

Her eyelids flickered, then her eyes opened, and she focused on the ceiling. She took a couple of light gasping breaths and then lay quietly.

"Detective Corning is here," Mr. Overstone said, caressing his wife's cheek. "Can you talk to him a moment?"

She turned her eyes toward her husband and gave him a weak nod and a slight smile.

Hank glanced at the stern face of the nurse, then leaned over toward the patient. "Mrs. Overstone, it's Detective Corning. Can you tell us who shot you?"

Mrs. Overstone's voice came out in a gravelly whisper. "Jake Lincoln."

Hank was taken aback. Somehow he hadn't expected that answer. "Are you sure?"

She nodded.

"Why?" Hank asked.

She shook her head. "Bank robbery."

The beeping life support system changed to a long screech and Hank stepped back. The nurse frantically waved them away. "Go now," she said, scurrying to the bedside.

Two more nurses appeared, and the room became a hive of activity. The cops and Mr. Overstone were steered out to the hallway by an attendant.

Hank had wanted to ask the woman a few more questions, but it appeared it wasn't going to be possible real soon. He glanced at Niles Overstone. The man had his eyes on the entranceway to his wife's room, panic gripping his face.

In a few moments, the reassuring sound of a steady beep beep came from the room, and Niles Overstone breathed a sigh of relief. For the time being, Mrs. Overstone would be all right.

Overstone turned to Hank, a deep frown darkening his face. "My wife said it was Jake Lincoln."

Hank nodded thoughtfully and spoke in a soothing voice to the distraught man. "We'll do our best to bring him in as soon as possible."

King stepped forward. "I'm not so sure your wife knew what she was saying. She appeared delusional right after she was shot, and she still might not be thinking straight."

Overstone gave King a black look. "My wife's not delusional," he said. "I talked to her earlier, and she knows where she is and what's going on."

King shrugged and stepped back, and Hank wondered why his partner was sticking up for Jake. Perhaps it was because King had taken a dislike for Overstone, expressing his doubt about the man's innocence on a couple of occasions.

As far as Hank was concerned, he had the word of the victim. It was the strongest evidence they had against his friend, and something he couldn't afford to disregard no matter what his personal feelings were.

A doctor stepped from the room, introduced himself to the cops, and spoke in a quiet voice. "I'm afraid I can't let you see Mrs. Overstone again right now. She's been through a lot, physically and emotionally, and reliving the traumatic events might've been too much for her in her weakened state."

"I understand, doctor," Hank said. He took a business card from his jacket pocket and held it out. "Please call me if she becomes stable. It's very important."

The doctor took the card, glanced at it, then dropped it into the pocket of his jacket. "I'll let you know, Detective." He put a hand on King's shoulder. "You'd better go now."

Hank and King left the area, leaving Overstone behind to talk with the doctor and worry about his wife.

CHAPTER 20

Wednesday, 9:05 a.m.

AS SOON AS ANNIE HAD gotten Matty off to school, she had sat at her desk and gone over the facts of the case. Half an hour later, she was still stumped. It seemed to her that, other than the unknown robber, the only people who might possibly know the real story were the Overstones.

She had called Jake a little earlier. He'd survived the night more comfortably in Sammy's hideout than he'd expected, and though the homeless man hadn't turned up a lead yet, Annie was pleased to hear her husband was optimistic and in good spirits.

Unlike the police, Annie knew her husband was innocent, and her objective was clear—to prove it. But with no leads to follow, it didn't look as easy as it sounded.

Jake was in the same boat, and right now all he could do was stay in hiding until either she or Sammy uncovered something he could run with.

She knew Hank would do the right thing, whatever that was. But with the cop determined to follow the evidence, and without a clear certainty of Jake's innocence, she was afraid Hank wasn't going to be asking the right questions of the right people.

Hank was stuck in a legal box, and his cop's mind wouldn't let him think outside of it.

It was up to Annie, and she couldn't afford to sit around and wait for something to happen; she had to be proactive.

Merrilla Overstone was her best bet, but Annie had no access to the woman. The nearest thing was Merrilla's husband. He had to know something—possibly some knowledge regarding the bank robbery his wife might've shared with him before she had been shot.

Whoever had robbed the bank had been an idiot for doing so. And he'd also been careless. Though the killer had been cold-hearted, would anyone foolish enough to rob a bank be concerned about eliminating a witness unless convinced the woman posed a threat? He'd only be putting himself in more danger, and it didn't seem plausible. Annie was betting there was more to it than that.

Other than Merrilla getting a vague view of the killer from across the room, there had to be another connection between the two.

Was it blackmail?

But blackmail seemed far-fetched. Surely Mrs. Overstone knew the small amount of the take from the robbery. Why would a woman who was financially comfortable risk herself by blackmailing someone for a measly couple of thousand dollars?

What was Annie missing? What were they all missing?

She decided to go for a drive and take her chances. Her objective was to get into the waiting room of the hospital ICU one way or another and pray she'd run into Niles Overstone.

Annie got her handbag and keys from the kitchen and, in a couple of minutes, was heading toward Richmond Hill General Hospital.

She drove into the guest parking lot, marveled at the exorbitant price of parking, and pulled into a spot a few rows away from the front doors. Then, grabbing her handbag, she got out and approached the building.

As she neared the entrance, she stopped short and ducked behind a pillar. Niles Overstone was inside the lobby in the company of a woman, and they were heading for the exit.

The pair came out the doors, down the steps, and moved along the front of the building to a spot fifty feet from the entrance. They stopped and, in a moment, a cloud of smoke wafted above their heads.

Overstone's back was to Annie, facing the woman, and faint sounds of their conversation reached her.

She approached casually and stopped beside them. "Good morning," she said, aiming a smile at Overstone.

The man glanced at Annie and nodded an indifferent hello, then turned back to his partner as if to resume their conversation.

"I'm Annie Lincoln," she said.

Overstone turned his head toward her, a strange look in his eyes. "I should've recognized you." Then he frowned and glared a moment before asking in a demanding tone, "What do you want?"

"I need to talk to you about your wife," Annie said.

Without moving his angry eyes from Annie's face, Overstone spoke. "Wanda, this is the wife of the man who shot Merrilla."

Wanda gasped and took half a step back. Annie looked at the woman, who scowled back at her. Probably in her midfifties, Wanda was a good hundred pounds overweight. Hair puffed up in a sixties-style hairdo made her round, fat face appear even chubbier. A cigarette was tucked between her stern lips, one eye half-closed to prevent the swirling smoke from blinding her.

The cigarette wobbled as she spoke, and her eyes flashed in anger. "How dare you even come close to us after what your husband did to my sister?"

Annie looked calmly at the incensed woman and held her cool. "Mrs. ...."

"Mrs. Tinker," the woman said. "As if it's any of your business."

Annie forced a calm smile. "Mrs. Tinker, I'm very sorry about your sister, but I have good reason to believe my husband wasn't involved."

Overstone crossed his arms and spoke. "My wife said it was him. That's good enough for me."

"And me," Mrs. Tinker chimed in. She raised her voice a couple of decibels and spoke in a mocking tone. "Of course, you'd stick up for your husband. Believing him with no proof."

"Like you're sticking up for your sister without proof?" Annie asked coolly.

Wanda Tinker popped the cigarette from her mouth and glared, unable to answer.

Annie turned to Overstone. "You said you should've recognized me. Why is that?"

Overstone frowned. "I've seen you on the news. Last week, my wife and I saw a story about you two. Claimed you were some kind of heroes." He leaned in toward her, his eyes growing dark. "But as it turns out, you're nothing but killers."

Annie wasn't getting anywhere by being nice. She decided to try a new tactic. "Mr. Overstone, your wife witnessed the bank robbery, and suddenly she's deeply involved in blackmail. How do you explain that?"

Overstone scowled. "She had nothing to do with blackmail."

"What about the text messages from her phone? And the phone calls to my husband?"

Overstone shrugged. "He must've been threatening her."

"If that's the case, why didn't she report it to the police, or at least tell you about it?"

"I ... I don't know," the man said, signs of confusion on his face. "Perhaps she was ... afraid to say anything."

"Mr. Overstone, your wife's more intelligent than that. By not saying anything, she puts herself in even more danger."

"Maybe she didn't have time."

Annie cocked her head. "But she had time to send and receive text messages and phone calls from the bank robber as well as from the person who shot her."

Overstone opened his mouth to speak and nothing came out. He closed it again and looked at Wanda.

Mrs. Tinker poked the cigarette back into her mouth and put her hands on her hips. "We don't know why she made those phone calls. But she knows what she saw and who shot her. She also knows your husband robbed the bank."

Annie disregarded Wanda's comment and turned back to Overstone. "Your wife claimed you were having an affair. She hired my husband to find out the truth."

"That's preposterous," Overstone said. "It's a ridiculous assertion your husband made up in a feeble attempt to cover himself. There's no truth to it. It only proves he's lying to you and to the police."

"And you don't think it's possible your wife was mistaken about who shot her?"

Overstone gave his head a vigorous shake. "Never."

"Then why'd she give my husband two thousand dollars?"

Overstone frowned. "That's more lies."

"Her fingerprints were on the envelope of money."

He gave an exasperated sigh. "I don't know what that means. Perhaps your husband was blackmailing Merrilla."

"Oh? And what could he be blackmailing her about? Does she have something to hide?"

Overstone looked at Wanda for some help, but the woman was at a loss for words.

The man's face flushed with anger. "I think you'd better go now."

Annie didn't move.

Wanda dropped her cigarette and ground it into the

sidewalk, then brushed past Annie and strode toward the hospital steps.

Overstone followed her, leaving Annie watching them go.

She understood Niles Overstone's anger. He believed his wife. But if he ever dared to doubt his wife's word, perhaps he'd see things more clearly.

Not that Merrilla Overstone was lying, but Annie firmly believed the woman was delusional.

But with the weight of evidence so firmly stacked against Jake, she understood the man's stubbornness. Given the same situation, Annie would no doubt feel the same.

She had hoped to come out of this awkward interview with something additional she could investigate. But with Niles Overstone refusing to budge, and with Wanda Tinker as his cheerleader, it had amounted to nothing more than an uncomfortable confrontation.

CHAPTER 21

Wednesday, 10:12 a.m.

WHEN HANK HAD LEFT the hospital, he'd been deeply disturbed. He'd hoped against all odds to hear Mrs. Overstone identify her shooter as anyone other than Jake. He still dared to hope she was delusional, or at least had been delusional when she'd spoken to him directly after being shot.

A couple more minutes with her at the hospital might've cleared up a whole lot of questions. Mainly, why?

It nagged at him continually, and perhaps only Merrilla Overstone knew the answer.

Hank sat in his car behind the precinct, running what little he knew of the case through his troubled mind.

He'd sent King to do what King did best. His partner was going to hit the streets, talk to some of his CIs, and see what he could do to dredge up a lead. If Jake was the shooter, he had to have gotten the gun from somewhere. It was a slim chance, probably futile, but there wasn't much else for King to do at the moment.

At the very least, someone might know where Jake was hiding out.

All the obvious places had been checked. Friends and family of both Jake and Annie had been visited. Jake wasn't dumb enough to take shelter in a spot Hank was aware of, and Hank had assumed any obvious avenue of investigation would be pointless.

He desperately wanted to find the man he hoped he could still call his friend.

And Jake had been a friend. Not only had Jake and Annie been indispensable to both him and RHPD in many investigations, but also, as long as Hank had known them, the pair had proven themselves loyal and caring.

When Hank had lost his six-month-old daughter many years ago, resulting in a broken marriage, their support had done more to help him through his heartbreaking ordeal than anything else. He'd leaned on them again years later when his parents died. Hank had been best man at their wedding. He'd been there when Matty was born, and he'd witnessed the look on Jake's face when he first held his new son.

Through thick and thin, and in spite of ups and downs throughout the years, their friendship had not only endured, but had grown.

There was no doubt arresting Jake would be a painful experience, but if the chance presented itself, he'd have no choice but to do the very thing he loathed.

If Jake was guilty of the accusations against him, he could

be anywhere. But, assuming Jake was innocent, Hank figured he'd be close by, doing whatever he could to get at the truth. That meant Jake would need some support. He could hardly depend solely on Annie. He'd never put her in that kind of danger and risk her being arrested as an accomplice.

He had to be with someone he knew—someone Hank didn't know.

Hank closed his eyes and rested his head back. There had to be an answer. After a while, he smiled grimly to himself, opened his eyes, and started the car. He had an idea.

A few minutes later, Hank pulled his vehicle to a stop on the shoulder of the road short of the Richmond River overpass. He stepped out, hopped over a railing, and faced the embankment that ran down and touched the river below.

And that's when he saw Jake.

His friend was sitting on the grass and leaning against a rock, his legs stretched out in front of him. He faced the river, his back to Hank.

He recalled that some time ago, a homeless man named Sammy had discovered a body and reported it. He'd gone on to aid Hank and the Lincolns further in their investigation. It'd slipped Hank's mind and, in hindsight, Hank recalled that Sammy and Jake had struck up a strange friendship at that time.

And now that Hank had found Jake, he almost wished he hadn't.

He stood still a moment, torn between calling for backup and trusting his friend to surrender on his own. The right thing, of course, was to call it in, but Hank couldn't bring himself to do it. This was all too personal for him—for both of them.

Hank trod with caution, struggling to remain quiet as he eased down the bank, avoiding loose rocks and gravel. Halfway down, his foot loosened a clump of dirt, setting off a small avalanche of stones and soil that tumbled to a grassy patch ten feet below.

Jake rolled to his feet, poised as if ready to run.

Hank held up a hand in front of him, palm out. "Jake, wait."

Jake stood upright, glanced down the riverbank toward freedom, then looked at Hank.

Hank moved down the bank a few more steps and stopped. "We need to talk."

Jake edged away.

By the time Hank reached flat ground, Jake had moved twenty feet away and turned back, and was now facing the cop.

Hank stood still a moment and faced his friend. This wasn't going to be easy. He knew Jake would never surrender without some assurance it was only temporary. And Hank couldn't give him that assurance.

Jake folded his arms. "I didn't do it, Hank. You know better than that. And if you can't trust me, then you can't trust anyone."

Hank turned his head and watched the river flow by a moment. A handful of minnows swam in safer waters near the shore. A wild duck moved about lazily a few yards away, free to do as it pleased. Hank was the one imprisoned—

caught in a wave of anguish, and he couldn't escape.

He turned back to face Jake, bit his lip, and moved his hand under his jacket. His fingers caressed his service weapon, then his hand tightened around the grip and remained still.

"I have to take you in, Jake," he said, hating every word that came from his mouth.

Jake shook his head, his eyes never wavering. "You're not gonna arrest me, Hank."

Hank blinked and hesitated.

Jake spoke. "Hank, it's not that I don't trust you to do your job properly and get to the bottom of it, but I have to be free to do this. I have to find out who set me up." He shrugged. "If you can't do it, that only leaves me."

Hank fingered the trigger of his gun.

"If I can't figure this out in a couple of days," Jake said, "I'll turn myself in. You have my word on it." He paused. "But to prove my innocence, I need to know what you know."

"Jake, I've searched desperately, and I haven't found anything to back up your story."

"It's not a story, Hank. It's the truth. And I need you to help me prove it."

"Merrilla Overstone said you shot her."

"She's delusional. Confused. I tried to help her, not hurt her."

"Jake, we've looked into Niles Overstone. He has a solid alibi and no motive. I can't see any way he might be involved.

And there's no evidence either one of them was having an affair."

Jake narrowed his eyes. "Hank, do I look stupid enough to be involved in this?"

"Of course not," Hank said. "That's what bothers me so much. Knowing you like I do, it's impossible, and yet ..."

"Hank, are you saying you have nothing you can tell me? Nothing at all that'll help me?"

Hank shook his head. "Nothing."

"Whatever happens here, I want you to promise you'll leave Sammy out of this. He believes me, and he's only trying to help."

"I won't touch Sammy," Hank said and shrugged. "Besides, he's not here and I haven't seen you with him. You only happen to be near where he lives."

Jake offered a slight smile of thanks.

"King's out there looking for anything he can find from his CIs," Hank said. "And I assume you have Sammy doing the same."

"He might be," Jake said. "If he is, it's because he wants to help me."

Hank nodded.

"Are you gonna let me go?" Jake asked.

"I still can't do that, Jake. You should know that."

"Are you gonna shoot me?"

"It won't come to that."

"Then I'm leaving," Jake said. He turned his back and strode up the riverbank.

Hank took a few steps forward, a shaky hand gripping his

weapon. Then he stopped, the gun remaining firmly in its holster as he watched his friend disappear from view.

Had he failed?

There was no doubt he'd failed to uphold his oath as a cop. But as a friend, he was bound by another oath, an unwritten one he found impossible to break.

CHAPTER 22

Wednesday, 10:56 a.m.

JAKE WAITED OUT OF sight a few minutes and then carefully worked his way back toward Sammy's castle. Hank was nowhere in sight. Jake climbed up the bank and poked his head over the concrete abutment to ensure the coast was clear. It was. The cop had gone.

He knew Hank was only doing his job, and once this was all over, he wouldn't hold it against his friend. Besides, Hank had let him go without much of an argument, and Jake had a suspicion the incident wouldn't appear anywhere in Hank's reports. There was a reason Hank had come alone.

To be safe, Jake would no longer be able to hide out with Sammy. He'd have to find a safe place—one Hank would never discover. The cop might not be so accommodating next time.

Sammy had left a couple of hours ago, determined to get some information that would help Jake. The man was certain somebody knew more than they were telling, and he was going to keep at it until convinced otherwise.

Jake wasn't so optimistic. Hank had said he had nothing that would help clear Jake. And when Jake had talked to Annie earlier, she'd had nothing to go on, either. Though he'd wracked his brain for the last twenty-four hours, he'd come up completely dry.

Annie had told him the news of his fugitive status still hadn't reached the press, so as long as he steered clear of cops, he should be free to come and go as he wished. And that's what he was going to do.

He ducked under the overpass, retrieved the beautiful pink bicycle Sammy had procured for him, and dragged it up to the street. He hopped on, feeling like a circus clown riding a miniature bike around the ring. His long legs buckled and stuck out at awkward angles, but he managed to stay upright and was soon pedaling like mad down the street.

Pulling into the nearest coffee shop, he was pleased to see they offered free Wi-Fi. He propped the bike against a brick wall, pulled his cap down low, and went inside and bought a coffee and a thick steak sandwich, giving him access to the Wi-Fi password.

He selected a booth in the corner, took a sip of coffee, and pulled the iPad out from behind his belt.

After a quick search, he found the address and phone number for Richmond Realty. He hesitated a moment, then pulled out the burner phone and dialed the listed number, asking for Niles Overstone.

The female receptionist gave a curt reply. "I'm sorry, but Mr. Overstone isn't in today."

"Do you know where he is?" Jake asked. "He's supposed to be showing me a house this morning."

He heard her fingernails tapping on her keyboard, then she said, "I don't see any appointments for today, although he's expected in briefly a little later. Perhaps there's been a mix-up in his schedule. Would you like his cell phone number?"

"No, thanks. I have it. What time are you expecting him?"

"Around noon, but it might be better if you call him yourself and confirm your appointment."

"I'll do that," Jake said and hung up.

He looked at his watch. He'd be able to finish his snack and get to Richmond Realty with time to spare.

According to Annie, Overstone had spent most of the previous day at the hospital. He hoped the man would show up at the office on time. It might be Jake's only chance to confront him.

He sipped his coffee and studied Overstone's smiling face from his web page profile, prominently featured on Richmond Realty's website. He looked pretty much the same as in the photo Merrilla had given him. One of the company's top realtors, his page boasted higher prices when you sell and lower when you buy. Jake didn't understand how you could have both.

He finished his meal, then went back outside and hopped on the bike, keeping an eye out for police as he sped down the street toward his destination. Half an hour later, he turned into Midtown Plaza and glanced around.

Richmond Realty operated from a storefront at the far end

of the plaza. Jake wheeled around behind the unit to the employee parking area, propped the bike against the end of a dumpster, and looked around.

A handful of parking slots were occupied, but since it was not yet noon, he crossed the wide lane and sat on a curb opposite the parking area and waited.

Fifteen minutes later, a white Lexus appeared. It pulled down the lane and into a parking slot, and Jake strained to see the driver. It was Overstone.

He hopped up and reached the side of the car as Niles Overstone stepped out. The man shut the door and turned around, startled to see someone standing in front of him.

Then Overstone recognized Jake and his eyes widened. He edged away, coming to a stop with his back against the car door. As the agitated man glanced around and looked for an escape route, Jake moved in, standing inches away.

Overstone cowered back. "What ... what're you doing here?"

Jake crossed his arms and glared. "I need to talk to you."

"What about? You ... you shot my wife. What do we have to talk about?"

"I didn't shoot your wife."

"And you robbed the bank."

Jake leaned in. "I didn't rob the bank."

"Merrilla told me she recognized the bank robber when his mask came off. He was looking right at her."

"Did she say it was me?"

Overstone frowned. "She didn't have to. I know it was you, and so do the police. And ... and there was a witness."

Jake backed up half a step. "Mr. Overstone, I didn't shoot your wife, and if you have any knowledge of who it might've been, then you'd better tell me." Jake paused. "Otherwise, the shooter's still out there somewhere, and he might be coming for you next."

"Why would anyone want me dead?" Overstone asked.

"Because he might think your wife told you who he was."

"Is that why you're here? To kill me now?"

Jake laughed. "I'm on your side, Overstone. If I wanted to kill you, would I be bothering to talk to you right now?"

Overstone gave Jake a dubious look, then reached a hand inside his jacket. "I'm calling the police," he said, removing a cell phone.

Jake put a hand on the phone, preventing Overstone from dialing. "Why're you so anxious to have me arrested? Mr. Overstone, did you shoot your wife? Or hire someone to do it?"

Overstone's frown deepened, and he pulled his hand free and stepped aside, keeping one eye on Jake while he dialed.

Jake shook his head and walked away. It would take the police a while to get here, so that didn't concern him. But what bothered him was Overstone wouldn't listen to reason, and there was no doubt in Jake's mind the man's life might be in danger.

He wheeled the bike out to the sidewalk and hopped on. Glancing back, he saw Overstone getting into his car. Jake assumed the man would lock his doors, cower in fear, and wait for the police.

If the killer eventually came after Overstone, would Jake

be the target of another frame job? That was something he couldn't help. As a fugitive, he had no way of establishing an alibi. It was a perfect storm, and Jake was caught in the middle of it with no means of protection.

Jake had gotten a good enough view of the killer as he watched him enter the Overstone house, and he was convinced it wasn't Niles Overstone himself. But he wasn't so convinced the man hadn't arranged his own wife's shooting. If that was the case, then was Overstone involved in the bank robbery as well?

Or, if what Overstone had said was true, that his wife had recognized the robber, then who could it be? What was the connection between Merrilla Overstone and the real killer?

Those were questions Jake had to find answers for. But he was severely hampered in his movement and, other than Overstone's possible involvement, he had no theory or suspects.

CHAPTER 23

Wednesday, 12:14 p.m.

ANNIE HUNG UP THE phone and slouched back in her swivel chair. They hadn't made much headway on proving Jake's innocence, and she was emotionally exhausted.

Jake had just called her and told her about his confrontation with Niles Overstone. Her encounter with the man earlier hadn't amounted to anything more than Jake's had. If Overstone was involved in something criminal, he was covering himself pretty well, playing the part of a distraught husband to perfection.

When the doorbell rang, she pushed back her chair and went to answer it. She pressed an eye to the peephole and frowned at the face of Lisa Krunk.

Annie opened the door. Lisa had an unusually pleasant look on her face. Annie couldn't help but notice the lack of a microphone that usually seemed to be permanently fastened to the newswoman's hand.

"Good afternoon, Annie," Lisa said, her lips curling into a sincere smile.

"You should call first."

Lisa's wide, smiling mouth widened even more. "I was in the neighborhood, and I saw a car in the driveway. Did you get a new vehicle?"

Annie suppressing a frustrated sigh. "Yes, it's new. What can I do for you?"

"I'd like to talk to you about the case you're working on."

"What case?"

"The Overstone shooting."

How could Lisa possibly know about that? She and Jake hadn't been publicly involved in any investigations regarding either the bank robbery or the shooting of Merrilla Overstone.

Annie leaned against the doorframe and crossed her arms. "What makes you think we're looking into that?" she asked.

A hint of a knowing smile appeared on Lisa's face. "I can't reveal my sources, but I've received certain information that proves you're not only looking into it, but you and Jake are both heavily involved."

Annie glanced toward the road. The Channel 7 Action News van was parked at the curb, and she could make out someone in the driver seat. If Lisa had been hoping for an interview, Don would've been right behind her, his camera ready to capture every word. Annie decided Lisa had something more in mind than an on-camera interview.

"Get to the point, Lisa. I have things to do."

Lisa disregarded the comment. "Can I come in a moment? I have a proposition for you."

Annie frowned at the woman and unfurled her arms. She stepped back and waved Lisa in, then led her into the living room and motioned toward the couch.

Lisa sat down, crossed her legs, and laid her hands in her lap. "It's about Jake," she said.

Annie sat in her armchair and looked at Lisa. "What about Jake?"

Lisa leaned forward and spoke in a hushed tone as if afraid someone was lurking nearby and listening in. "I have a source who revealed to me Jake's a wanted fugitive. Wanted for the bank robbery as well as for the shooting of Merrilla Overstone." She sat back, a smug look on her face. "I thought we could make a deal."

Annie stared at Lisa a moment. The nosy newswoman had eyes and ears everywhere. There wasn't much that escaped her when she put her mind to a task. "Where did you hear that?" Annie asked.

Lisa pointed out the window to Annie's car. "I saw Hank going over your Toyota yesterday. I didn't realize it was yours at the time, but I got the idea it was involved somehow." She shrugged. "It's true, isn't it? Jake's a fugitive."

Annie didn't answer, wondering if Lisa was making assumptions and digging for information.

Lisa continued, "I've known you and Jake for a long time, and though this would make a great story, I happen to think Jake's innocent." She let out an exaggerated sigh, a pained expression on her face. "I couldn't bring myself to run with it." She paused and unconsciously brushed a hand through her short black hair. "I owe you two a small favor, anyway."

"You owe us a small favor?" Annie asked. "You mean, for saving your life?"

Lisa smiled. "It's the least I could do." She cleared her throat. "As you know, Annie, millions of people tune into the news every day to watch my stories."

Annie refrained from rolling her eyes and waited for Lisa to continue.

"So in return for me keeping quiet about Jake—"

"What happened to the favor?"

"That's part of it," Lisa said.

Annie didn't argue. It made no sense, but according to Lisa's one-sided logic, it made all the sense in the world. Lisa seemed determined to come out the big winner in any deal.

"When this is all over," Lisa continued, "I'd like to do a one-hour special on Jake's story. I think it would make a great human-interest piece, and my watchers would be overjoyed when I reveal how one man, with the help of his faithful wife, triumphed over impossible odds."

Lisa seemed to have the tagline written already. She'd probably been working on it all day.

"And what if it doesn't end the way you expect?" Annie asked.

Lisa smiled knowingly.

"Is there something you're not telling me?"

The newswoman shook her head and raised her thinly plucked eyebrows. "Nothing at all. I have faith in you two."

"I can't speak for Jake," Annie said. "The choice'll have to be his." She didn't want to admit Jake was a fugitive, but she was becoming more and more convinced Lisa was sincere and had her facts straight.

"Look at it as a business decision," Lisa continued. "I'm sure you could always use the positive exposure. It would be very good for Lincoln Investigations."

"Perhaps it would, but it's a personal matter, and Jake would have to okay it."

Lisa raised her chin and smiled. "Give me your word you like the idea and you'll try to convince your husband. I happen to know Jake doesn't take much convincing as far as you're concerned."

Lisa was right about that. Jake was a pushover when it came to her, but she didn't want to take advantage of him. Nonetheless, if the deal kept the public from being aware of what was going on, it was a good thing.

"You have my word," Annie said. "I'll talk to Jake about it."

Lisa smiled.

"On one condition," Annie continued. "If the public becomes aware the police are hunting for Jake, whether or not the information comes from you, the deal's off."

"Fair enough," Lisa said.

"Are you going to tell me your source?" Annie asked, knowing it was a futile question.

"I can't do that, Annie. You know better than to ask."

"Normally, I wouldn't ask," Annie said. "But if it helps me get to the bottom of this, I'd appreciate anything you can give me."

Lisa paused, then spoke flatly. "Telling you my source won't help you."

"Is there anything else you know that might?"

Lisa narrowed her eyes and stared at Annie as she considered the question. Finally, she said, "I don't know how relevant it is, and it's going to come out in my story this evening, but Niles Overstone mentioned to me his wife's dying of cancer. According to him, she might only have a short time left, and he wants the world to know."

Though Annie wasn't sure how useful it was, the revelation was surprising, and she wondered if Hank was aware of it. She'd have to give the information some thought and run it by Jake later.

"Anything else?" she asked.

Lisa shook her head. "I don't believe so. Just some sketchy information from witnesses at the bank robbery. If properly edited, it'll add some interest to my piece, but there's nothing in their stories that means anything as far as reliable evidence is concerned."

"If you come across something, don't keep it from me," Annie said. "Anything that helps Jake out is good for everyone."

"I won't," Lisa said, and Annie decided the newswoman was telling the truth. Lisa appeared to want Jake's story badly, and Annie knew she'd do just about anything in her power to make it happen.

"Have you been in contact with Jake?" Lisa asked.

"I can't tell you that."

Lisa smiled knowingly. "I'll take that as a yes." She paused and gave a short laugh. "That was my curiosity as a newsperson. I had to ask."

Annie stood. "If there's nothing else, Lisa, I have some things I have to do."

Lisa stood, brushed down the wrinkles in her blouse, and offered Annie a genuine smile. "That's all for now."

Annie saw her to the door and let her out.

The newswoman turned her head and called over her shoulder as she headed down the pathway to her van, "Give my regards to Jake."

Annie closed the door and hoped she'd done the right thing in making the promise to Lisa. She decided she had. Lisa wanted Jake's story, and instead of the woman causing trouble, as was characteristic of her, it was good to have her on their side for a change. That meant one less problem to overcome, and for all she knew, it might help.

CHAPTER 24

Wednesday, 1:28 p.m.

JAKE WORKED THE bicycle behind a hedge at the rear of a strip plaza not far from Richmond Realty. He concealed it as well as he could with dead leaves and branches and stood back. It would be safe there for the time being.

He might come back for the bike later, but it was becoming more of an annoyance than useful transportation, drawing looks from curious drivers and amused smiles from pedestrians. With his long legs, he could make just about the same speed. And anyway, he had nowhere to be at the moment.

He crossed the street to a grassy area near a towering office building facing Main Street, then sat and leaned against a shade tree. He played the little talk he'd had with Overstone over in his mind for the umpteenth time.

Pedestrians hurried up and down the sidewalk, cars sped by on the street, and furry animals played in the bushes nearby. It seemed like he was the only one without real freedom.

The cell phone in his back pocket rang, and he answered it. Other than Sammy, Annie was the only person with his number, and he was happy to hear her cheerful voice, even if it appeared forced. Though not hampered by the law on her heels, he knew she had to be going through as much as he was.

"Lisa was here," Annie said.

"Oh? Causing more problems?"

Annie explained the proposition the newswoman had presented to her. "I know it's not something you want to think about right now," she said. "But I had to see how you're doing, anyway."

"I'm doing great," Jake said, knowing it was a half-truth. "And tell Lisa I'll do the interview. As long as it helps me move around more safely, it's no big deal to me. She can have whatever she wants."

"She also told me Merrilla Overstone's dying of cancer," Annie said. "According to Niles Overstone, his wife might have only a short time left."

"Cancer?" Jake said. "Overstone didn't mention that to me."

Annie chuckled. "You two aren't exactly on the best of speaking terms. Why would he?"

"No reason, I guess. He seemed more concerned with calling the cops on me. I didn't get anything from him, anyway. If he knows anything about the bank robbery or his wife's shooting, he never gave me any hint."

"Other than your talk with Overstone, have you found out anything else?" Annie asked.

"Not a thing. I'm still waiting to hear from Sammy, and I'm also hoping you'll find a lead. I'm tired of not knowing what's going on, and I need to get digging into this thing."

"It'll come," Annie said. "Up until now, Hank's been forthcoming with me, and I keep in touch with him." She paused, then said, "We miss you here, but you'd better go. You don't want to kill the charge in your cell phone. And I'm going to be doing some snooping around this afternoon, and I'll call you if I find out anything."

"Be careful, and I miss you, too," Jake said, then hung up and glanced at the phone. He still had a half charge. He tucked it into his back pocket, then pulled his cap low and dropped his head when a police car drove by. The officer had his head halfway out the window, craning his neck as he peered to get a better view.

Jake decided he'd better scram.

Too late.

The cruiser came to a quick stop, and the officer jumped out. Jake sprang to his feet and headed for the rear of the apartment building. He spun around the corner and poked his head back around.

The pursuing cop was fast, and his beltload of goodies didn't seem to be slowing him down. One hand was on his two-way radio, no doubt calling for backup. The cruiser had disappeared.

He turned and ran down the back of the apartment building toward an adjoining side street. He assumed the cop car would be circling the block in an attempt to cut him off, and he hoped to get past the danger area before the cruiser appeared.

By the time he touched the street, the cop on foot had rounded the building and was not far behind.

"Police! Stop! Put your hands up!"

He wasn't about to do that.

To his left, the cruiser sped up the street, its lights flashing, its siren off. It would soon be on him if he didn't make tracks. The vehicle screeched to a stop as Jake leaped over a hedge and scurried down the side of a house.

Now both cops were on foot, and backup would be on the way—perhaps even ahead of him, anticipating his next move.

He couldn't hide. The area would be thoroughly searched, and he'd be discovered. He had to hurry and get out of there before it was too late. Maybe he should've hung onto the bicycle a little longer.

Perhaps he could find another one.

Or better yet ...

Jake tore past the house and landed on the sidewalk of the next side street. He glanced in both directions, then took a right and circled back to Main. A choir of sirens sounded in the distance. Backup was coming—more than one car—and they weren't far away.

"Police! Stop!"

It came from behind him. His pursuers weren't getting

closer, but they weren't giving up, either. His one advantage was they would never shoot an unarmed man in the back. As long as he kept ahead of them, he'd be safe.

But if he didn't do something quickly, and maybe something drastic, he'd soon be outnumbered and surrounded.

He took another right turn at Main and beat a furious path down the sidewalk, tearing past startled pedestrians and dodging obstacles. He'd circled the block. It didn't really matter where he ran, as long as he kept out of the arms of the law. And soon those arms would be everywhere.

And then, dead ahead, he saw his way out.

As he ran, he stuffed a hand into his pocket and pulled out the roll of bills. He peeled off two hundred dollars, shoved the rest back into his pocket, and folded the bills up in his fist.

He ground to a quick stop beside a startled man in the process of kick-starting his motorcycle. The man's head spun toward Jake, and his eyes widened.

"Sorry," Jake said. "I need your bike."

With one huge fist, Jake grabbed a handful of the back of the man's leather jacket and lifted him clear off the motorcycle. He planted the frightened man onto his feet beside the bike, smoothed down the guy's jacket, and offered him a friendly grin.

"You'll get your bike back," Jake said. "I'll take good care of it."

He pressed the bills into the man's hand, then leaped onto the bike and kicked it into gear.

"You can pick it up at the police station," Jake yelled over the roar of the engine. "Thanks for the loan."

He left the man with his mouth hanging open and pulled from the curb. He took a look over his shoulder. The pursuing cops were close, but they were going to be too late. He swerved into traffic and glanced in the mirror, smiling grimly to himself as the cops on foot came to a stop beside the confused man.

Sirens were blaring not far behind, cruiser drivers undoubtedly aware of the current situation. Cops would be leaning over their steering wheels, probably chomping at the bit, eager to be the one who marched the fugitive into the precinct.

But it wasn't gonna happen if Jake could help it.

He edged between two lanes crammed with vehicles waiting at a red light. Coming to a stop, he tightened his fingers around the grips, ready to run the light if he found himself in danger of being nabbed.

The light changed green and the bike leaped off the line.

Sirens screeched in his ear, almost on him now. Cars pulled to the side in front and behind to make way for the pursuing vehicles.

But police cars, even with the best drivers, were no match for a motorcycle on city streets. Especially if Jake was driving.

With cruisers at his heels, he swerved to the right, leapfrogged the curb, then sped down an alley between two storefronts.

He spun onto a service road behind the building, spitting up loose stones as he veered left, then quickly approached another side street. Crossing over, he took an access lane behind a line of stores and continued on, the screech of sirens now fading.

After a couple more minutes, he'd put a safe distance between himself and the sure-to-be-frustrated cops.

CHAPTER 25

Wednesday, 3:11 p.m.

HANK HAD SPENT THE last four hours conducting a second interview with anyone remotely involved in either the bank robbery or the shooting of Merrilla Overstone. Whether or not Jake was involved, the detective had been hoping to find the one tidbit of information to break the case wide open.

King had been on the streets talking to any of his CIs who had connections to the seedier side of the city. Most of his CIs were known to be in the drug world, but where there was a buck to be had, a handful of his criminal connections had their claws everywhere, spreading their expertise among a variety of unlawful acts.

Both detectives had come up empty-handed.

News of the near capture of Jake had spread throughout the precinct. Hank knew many had silently cheered when they heard Jake had eluded arrest, but he also knew not everyone in local law enforcement called themselves a friend of the Lincolns. Whether it was jealously due to the Lincolns' relationship with RHPD, or something else, Hank didn't know, but there was no doubt that an undeniable trace of resentment toward his friends existed in the department.

Hank didn't know exactly where he stood on the near miss. A part of him wanted to see Jake brought in; he just didn't want to be the one to do it.

But right now, he had a lot of paperwork to do—a mundane task that kept him from doing what he really wanted to get at.

He looked up as Officer Spiegle weaved his way through the maze and approached Hank's desk, his usual cheery face now sporting a serious expression.

"What is it, Yappy?"

"Diego wants to see you and King," the young cop said.

Hank glanced toward Diego's open office door. The captain's door was always open. Though he could be tough when he needed to be, he had the backs of those who called him Captain, and he'd earned the respect of the men and women who enforced the law under his command.

"Thanks, Yappy," Hank said. "Do you wanna see if you can round up King?" He jerked a thumb over his shoulder. "Last I saw him, he was heading for the break room."

"I'll get him," Yappy said, scurrying away.

A minute later, King approached Hank, and the two cops headed for Diego's office. The captain was hunched over his desk, involved in some paperwork. Hank tapped on the door and Diego looked up.

"You wanted to see us, Captain?" Hank asked.

Diego sat back, pushed his paperwork aside, and waved them in.

Hank sat in the guest chair and stretched out his legs. King leaned in his usual place, holding up the filing cabinet, his arms crossed.

The captain stroked his dark mustache, then laid his arms on the armrest and observed Hank a moment before speaking.

"I'm a little concerned about the both of you, but mainly you, Hank," Diego said, his jowls quivering as he talked. "I know how close you are to the Lincolns, and I have serious issues with you concerning this case."

Hank frowned. "What kind of issues, Captain?"

"Frankly, I'm not sure how well you can do your job." Diego paused and straightened his tie, then cleared his throat before continuing, "I'd be lying if I said this case didn't disturb me, as well. I have a soft spot for Jake and Annie. You know that, Hank. But I have to do my job, and so do both of you."

"I'm doing my job, Captain," Hank said. "As close as this is to me, I can't let personal relationships get in my way."

"Diego glanced at King a moment, then back at Hank, and waved a hand toward the precinct floor. "I understand that, Hank, but you're under scrutiny. Not only by me, but by many out there. If it turns out Jake's involved in these crimes, IA might take a hard look at it simply because of your involvement." Diego narrowed his eyes. "And you know how they can be. Sometimes they've nothing better to do, and even the slightest indication of impropriety on your part could mean a serious reprimand, perhaps even your job."

King shuffled his feet uneasily and recrossed his arms.

"And that goes for you, too, King," Diego said. "Watch your butts, both of you."

"So you're not pulling us off?" Hank asked, half-wishing the captain would've removed him from the case. He was having his own serious doubts about how well he could do his job.

"Of course not. Consider this a warning," Diego said. He leaned forward and held up a finger. "Not because I have any suspicions of misconduct by either one of you, but you're both good cops, and this is a touchy matter."

The captain glared long and hard at King a moment, then sat back and crossed his arms above his ample belly. He took a deep breath, and his demeanor relaxed. "So, where are we on this case?"

Hank looked at King, and King looked back at Hank.

Hank took a breath. "We haven't made a lot of headway," he said. "But we're following the evidence, and most of it leads to Jake. We have his story, and it all fits, but the evidence says otherwise."

"I've gone over his story as well," Diego said. "I'm not saying he's innocent, but assuming for a second he is, do you have anything at all that gives him the benefit of the doubt?"

"He had no motive," Hank said. "That's the strongest defense I can give him right now."

"Assuming his motive isn't money, then," Diego said, "what does Jake stand to gain by any of this?"

"Nothing to gain, Captain, and everything to lose."

"Nothing obvious, at least," King put in. "We can't find any prior connection between Jake and either of the Overstones."

"Or the woman killed at the bank," Hank added. "Or anyone else remotely involved."

"Keep digging," Diego said. "Dig long and hard. If he had any motive at all, no matter how obscure, I want to know about it."

"You got it, Captain."

"In the meantime," Diego continued, "we have to bring Jake in no matter what. He'll get a fair trial, there's no doubt about that, but we have to find him."

"We're trying," King said. "And so are the officers on the street."

Diego steepled his fingers under his chin and looked at Hank over top. "What about Annie?"

"What about her, Captain?"

"Have you talked to her?"

"She's Jake's wife," Hank said. "She's standing by him."

"Keep in touch with her," Diego said. "She's as smart as a whip, and she's the only one fully convinced of Jake's innocence. If she comes up with something to help Jake's case, you have my support to pursue it. But it has to be something convincing. You have a job to do."

"We'll do our job, Captain. Finding out the truth, no matter how troubling it is, is what we're sworn to do."

Diego nodded. "Then do it. Bring Jake in, or prove him innocent. Or both, but keep me informed."

Hank stood. "You got it, Captain."

"Go," Diego said, dismissing them with a wave. He pulled a file folder toward him and flipped it open.

King followed Hank back to his partner's desk and dropped into the guest chair. "You got any ideas, Hank?"

Hank shook his head and sat down. "I'd really like to talk to Merrilla Overstone again, but it doesn't look like it's gonna happen anytime soon." He paused and cocked his head at King. "What about you?"

"Word on the street is somebody else is asking questions. Not sure who it is. It might be Jake, but nobody I talked to seems to know anything about either shooting."

"Are you offering enough?"

"I've promised them money as well as favorable consideration in any future charges against them. Believe me, if my guys knew something, they'd spill it."

"I'm gonna hit the streets myself a little later," Hank said. "There're a few guys I can talk to." He paused. "The thing that concerns me is, if these crimes were carried out by a two-bit hood, there's always information to be had. But when nobody knows a thing, it makes it look like the perp isn't one of the regular street punks."

"Doesn't look good for Jake," King said. "But it doesn't prove anything."

"It doesn't help, either," Hank said. "And right now, nothing seems to be helping."

CHAPTER 26

Wednesday, 4:07 p.m.

ANNIE HAD A THEORY, and she wanted to prove it. Anxious to see where it led, she called Chrissy and asked her to watch Matty for an hour or two. Her friend was home and said it would be no problem. The boys were in the backyard, and after notifying Matty she'd be out for a while, Annie grabbed her handbag along with a few things she might need and hurried to her car.

As she pulled from the driveway and drove down the street, she kept an eye in her rearview mirror. No one appeared to be following her this time. They might've learned their lesson before, or perhaps they were being more cautious. She'd need to be careful, as well. What she was about to do wasn't exactly legal.

She had hoped to have access to their garage by now, giving her the ability to lock her car inside. Though it seemed like a long shot, there was always a chance someone in law enforcement might have the bright idea of putting a tracker on her vehicle. But Jake's Firebird occupied the single-car garage, and due to the evidence found inside the building, legal entry was denied to her for the time being.

After driving around the block, she backtracked her route a couple of times, and in a few minutes, she pulled to the curb in front of the Overstone house. She was satisfied no one had been tailing her, but she had no way of knowing whether or not some eager cop was parked elsewhere at this very moment, aware of her every movement. It was a chance she had to take.

She glanced at the house. Crime scene tape crisscrossed the front door, fluttering in the afternoon breeze. The rear door would be sealed as well, and the yellow tape assured her the house would be empty, its owner still not allowed access to the residence.

After waiting a couple more minutes, she got out of her car and glanced around. The residential street was quiet, most of the homeowners still at work. She strode up the sidewalk, crossed the front of the house to the right side, then took a wide grassy pathway leading between the two properties.

She studied the side of the house. A window led into the living room, a lower one into a darkened basement. She tested both windows. They were firmly locked.

Going to the back corner, Annie peered around and glanced across the rear of the house. A waist-high hedge separated the property from the one next door, a row of bushes lining the back of the quarter acre of land.

She eased around the corner and crouched down, testing

another basement window. It was secure as well, and Annie was beginning to doubt her theory.

Then, moving across the back of the house, she climbed the steps to a small deck. Her eyes widened. A woman lounged in a deck chair next door. Annie ducked down and held her breath, her side view of the woman's head and shoulders now obscured by the hedge. She waited a moment and prayed she hadn't been seen or heard.

Reaching up with one hand, Annie gently brushed the crime scene tape aside and twisted the knob. The door was securely locked. She'd expected that.

Keeping low, she eased off the deck and tiptoed to the corner of the house. A vague outline of the neighbor was visible through the thinning bushes, the woman's back now toward Annie.

Then, creeping up the side of the house, Annie poked at the final window leading into the basement. It opened an inch, then slapped back against the frame.

Holding her breath, she glanced around, then pushed on the window frame. The window swung upwards, clicked into place, and stayed open.

She leaned over and squinted into the dim basement, then, feet first, she eased through the window and dropped to the concrete floor.

Annie strained to see by the faint light streaming through the open window, then rifled through her handbag and removed a small flashlight. She flicked it on and shone it around. To her right, a row of shelving held a stack of magazines and cardboard boxes of all shapes and sizes. Other

172

junk was heaped in a corner. On the far side of the room, a set of stairs led to the main floor.

She eased around a washing machine, navigated past a stack of boxes, then reached the stairs and looked up. The door at the top yawned open.

Annie climbed the stairs, stepped into the kitchen, and looked at her surroundings. The floor had been cleaned where she imagined the victim's blood had been spilled. The rest of the room was tidy, probably exactly how it'd been before the fateful incident.

According to Hank, jewelry and other valuable items had been found where they should be, and the presumption had been that the home hadn't been burglarized. Annie felt sure the intruder's intention had been solely to kill Mrs. Overstone and get out of there.

But where did Jake fit into the picture?

Annie wandered into the living room, where light streamed through sheers covering a large front window. The room was immaculate. Photos lined the mantel above the fireplace, and more were on end tables, all featuring smiling images of better days. Plants were drooping on the coffee table. The hardwood floor was clean and gleamed in the sunlight.

She went into an office leading off the hallway. A faint smell of perfume hung in the air. Removing a pair of gloves from her handbag, she rummaged through a filing cabinet. It contained nothing more than carefully filed receipts for bills and mortgage payments, all neatly labeled, categorized, and tucked safely into manila folders.

She turned and flashed the light around the room. A bookcase contained rows of novels. A few prints hung on the brightly painted walls. The desk was organized and clean, a smiling photo of Niles Overstone prominently displayed. Pulling open the top drawer, she saw the usual assortment of necessities—a stapler, tape, pens, and pencils.

A side drawer in the desk appeared to be empty. It seemed unusual, so she flicked on her flashlight, knelt down, and peered inside. There was no doubt it was totally bare. The drawer seemed to be a snug fit, but she managed to work it closed, then she shone the flashlight around the room, taking another quick look before heading for the door.

She stopped, thought a moment, then went back to the desk and opened the side drawer again. Sliding back a clip on either side, she tugged the drawer completely out, then set it on the floor and knelt down. She directed her light inside and smiled grimly.

A small envelope was taped to the floor of the cavity. She worked the packet loose, stood, and turned it over in her hands. There was no writing on the package, but after shaking it, she was pretty sure she knew what it contained. She flipped open the envelope and peered inside. It held a pair of keys.

Safe deposit box keys.

Annie stared at them a moment. The box they unlocked might contain something valuable, and perhaps invaluable to the investigation. But what could she do with them? She'd have no legal access to the box. Only the police could do that, and she wasn't about to tell Hank she'd broken into the Overstone house.

There wasn't much point in putting them back. The investigators had missed them the first time, and it was doubtful they would do a second search.

Did Niles Overstone know about the existence of these keys? Perhaps he'd put them there, but Annie assumed Merrilla had hidden them. The feminine touches in the office made her suspect the wife took care of the family business, and it was likely Merrilla's desk and her keys.

Annie dropped the envelope into her handbag, replaced the drawer, and left the office, hoping she'd discovered something useful.

After a quick look around the second floor of the house, she left through the basement window and peeked through the hedge. The woman still sat in her chair next door, engrossed in a magazine or paperback.

Annie hurried to her car.

The intention of her excursion to the Overstone house had not been to discover any new evidence. The keys had been a bonus. Her plan had been to work on her theory, and she now felt she'd been correct.

Whoever had shot Mrs. Overstone had hurried down to the basement after the shooting, then had left through the basement window, with no choice but to leave it unlocked.

She was sure the gunman had fully expected Jake to go into the house after hearing the shot. Then the would-be killer had planted the burner phone with the incriminating text message under the seat of the Toyota and erased the pictures on the camera.

It seemed like it had been a risky undertaking, but if

everything went as planned, Jake would be the perfect suspect.

Had Jake been set up intentionally, or had he fallen neatly into the killer's scheme merely by being there when it had all gone down?

Her theory made perfect sense, though Annie still didn't know why Merrilla Overstone had been a target.

On the way home, she wracked her brain to come up with a way of getting the keys to Hank without him knowing of her involvement.

There was only one sure and safe way.

She arrived home and hurried into the office, then stuffed the packet of keys into an envelope and, disguising her handwriting, she addressed it to RHPD in care of Detective Hank Corning.

She'd been careful not to get her fingerprints on the envelope, but probably with a little detective work, Hank could trace it back to her. Undoubtedly, he'd suspect where it had come from, but Annie assumed he wouldn't bother tracking down the source once he found out what it contained.

She drove to the corner, dropped the envelope into a mailbox, and returned home.

Hank should get it by the next morning, and she was eager to find out where it might lead.

CHAPTER 27

Wednesday, 5:12 p.m.

JAKE WROTE A NOTE requesting the motorcycle be returned to its owner, then attached the note to the bike and parked it outside the fire station. That was the best he could do. He wasn't about to go near RHPD right now, and he was sure the bike would safely find its way home before long.

He went into a sports shop and bought a new baseball cap and a white t-shirt, dumping his old cap and black shirt into the nearest garbage container. No doubt the officers who'd chased him would've radioed in his description. It wasn't much of a disguise, but he figured it might make the difference between being noticed by another eagle-eyed cop or not.

He wandered down the busy street, approaching the downtown core. Office buildings shot up everywhere. Hard-working folks were getting off work, and people bustled all around him in their haste to get somewhere important. What better place to hide than in plain sight?

When his burner phone rang, he stopped and answered it. It was Sammy, and the homeless man announced he had some good news.

"The guy you're looking for is Dewey Hicks," Sammy said. "As far as I could find out, he was boasting to some of the other punks about setting you up."

"Amazing, Sammy," Jake said. "Where can I find this guy?"

"I don't know, Jake. All I can tell you is he hangs around with a nasty crowd. Shouldn't be too hard to find, though. Apparently, he's pretty well known among the two-bit criminals."

"Any idea what he looks like?"

"Can't help you with that."

"Anything else you can tell me?"

"You might try some of the dive bars downtown. Ask around. You got any money left?"

"A couple hundred."

"That'll open their mouths. I expect there's not a lot of loyalty with that bunch." Sammy paused, then added, "But be careful, Jake. You look too much like a cop, and most of them don't talk to cops. You gotta find the right guy."

"I'll figure it out. Thanks, Sammy. I'll let you know what I come up with."

"Good luck."

Jake hung up the phone and stuffed it into his back pocket. Finally, he had a lead, and he was determined to find the punk named Dewey Hicks.

He just didn't know where to start.

But he had an idea. Sammy had said he looked like a cop, and there really wasn't any way around it. No matter what he did, he could never disguise himself to look like one of the street punks, and besides, most of them probably knew each other in one way or another. He'd stick out like a sore thumb.

There was only one answer. If he looked like a cop, he'd have to find a way to take advantage of it.

He headed for the fetid backstreets of the older downtown area, where dive bars and hangouts proliferated, hoods hung out on every dimly lit corner, and the tumbledown housing contained the poor, the homeless, and the downtrodden.

A lowlife gave Jake a wary eye when he stopped in front of a dive bar and peered through the grimy window. Half a dozen patrons lounged at tables, while the bartender wiped down the bar with a beer-stained cloth.

Jake moved on and wandered down the next side street. The area was littered with dingy storefronts, owners trying their best to scrape out a living.

Like frightened mice, a couple of delinquents scurried back into an alley when Jake approached.

What were they afraid of?

Jake wanted to find out.

He hurried forward and peered down the alley in time to see the punks scramble through a doorway and disappear.

Jake followed and came to a stop in front of a battered door. He pushed at the door, and it swung open. A stale smell wafted from the narrow hallway. A dusty light bulb allowed barely enough light to see.

He stepped inside. To his right, a metal door was locked securely, probably the rear entrance to one of the many storefronts that lined the street.

Further down, other doors led off to the right, one door to the left, perhaps into an apartment. That had to be where the hoods had gone.

Jake eased down the hallway and stopped in front of the door. He twisted the knob. It was locked.

Hoping there was no back way out, Jake banged on the door. There was no answer, and he stared at the door a moment. Should he break it down?

"Open the door," he yelled, banging again.

The door opened as far as the security chain would allow, and one of the punks stuck his nose out.

"What d'you want? We ain't done nothing wrong."

"Then you won't mind letting me in."

"Got a warrant?"

Jake shrugged. "Who needs a warrant? If I had a warrant, I'd have to search the place. You wouldn't want that, would you?"

The hood's small brain seemed to be churning. Finally, he closed the door, removed the chain, then scraped the door all the way open.

The guy moved back and Jake stepped into the filthy room. Stale cigarette smoke mixed with the odor of a freshly lit joint. Faint music played from a cheap stereo somewhere in the other room.

The second hood was in a combination bedroom-kitchen, a scowl on his face as he wiped a hand on his grimy t-shirt and looked at Jake.

"I know you guys are selling," Jake said. He gave the second hood the once-over, taking in the greasy hair that dripped down onto his shoulders, his worn-out jeans, and the cocky look on his boyish face. Both guys were in their early twenties, and Jake wondered how two young lives could go so wrong.

Punk number one looked bewildered. "You ain't never bothered us before." He looked at his companion and then back at Jake, a pained expression on his face. "It's just a bit of weed."

"Sorry, can't help it. The captain told us to crack down. Some kind of blitz to keep the mayor happy. There's an election coming up, you know." Jake shrugged. "I gotta do what I gotta do."

The guy swore. "I ain't heard nothin' about that."

"Can't help what you didn't hear," Jake said. "I gotta run you two guys in."

The guy frowned and peered out into the hallway. "Where's your partner?"

"Getting his hand looked after. He almost broke a finger on some idiot's face a few minutes ago."

The guy scowled. "We ain't carrying nothing."

"You want me to search your place?"

The man shook his head.

"Maybe I can help you outta this," Jake said. "I hear you been getting Oxy from Dewey Hicks."

A deep frown twisted the punk's face. "Dewey don't sell Oxy."

Jake leaned in and glared, towering over the frightened

man by almost twelve inches. "You want outta this or not?"

The guy looked up with eager eyes and nodded vigorously.

The other hood moved closer. "Don't tell him nothing, Mikey. Dewey'll plug us full of holes."

"You don't have to snitch on Hicks," Jake said. "Tell me where to find him, and I'll put in a good word for you guys with the captain."

"You won't tell Dewey we talked to you?" Mikey asked.

Jake straightened up. "I won't say a word, Mikey. Hicks is the guy we really want."

Mikey glanced at the other punk and received a shrug in return. He crossed his arms, leaned against the wall, and squinted up at Jake. "What's in it for us? Could be big trouble if Dewey finds out about this."

"You get to keep your freedom," Jake said. He folded his hand into a massive fist and held it in front of Mikey's nose. "Besides, who could do more damage to that pretty face of yours, Hicks, or me?"

Mikey looked cross-eyed at the fist and bit his lip.

"Better tell him, Mikey," lowlife number two said in a sighing voice.

Jake grabbed a handful of Mikey's t-shirt. "I advise you to do as your friend says."

Mikey took a deep breath and spoke, almost spitting out the words. "When he ain't on a gig, Dewey hangs out at Gully's most of the time."

"Who's Gully?"

"Gully's Bar. Over on Chester Street." Mikey shook his head. "But Dewey don't sell Oxy. He's not into drugs. Mostly breaking into places and stuff. I'm telling you, if you're looking for narcos, you got the wrong guy."

Jake let go of Mikey's shirt and smoothed it into place. "We'll see, Mikey. Word is he's taking over drugs in the area."

Mikey gave Jake a dubious look and then took a sideways step. "You'll leave us be now?"

"As long as you aren't lying to me, you have nothing to worry about." Jake pointed a finger at Mikey's nose. "You don't want me to have to come back."

Mikey shook his head.

Jake glared at the other punk a moment, then turned and stepped into the hallway. The door closed behind him, the chain rattled, and Jake smiled grimly to himself.

Now all he had to do was find Dewey Hicks and make him talk.

CHAPTER 28

Wednesday, 6:00 p.m.

LISA KRUNK STOOD in the wings of the Channel 7 Action News studio and watched the monitor as teasers ran for upcoming news stories. Her piece would be the lead, as usual, and though it was bound to be compelling due to her expertise in bringing the public stories they yearned for, it wasn't as groundbreaking as she'd hoped.

She was having second thoughts about her deal with Annie. There was no doubt in her mind revealing Jake as a wanted fugitive would've rocked the city, and rocking the city was what she did best. And if one of the other news outlets happened across the information and released it to the public, for the time being, she'd look like a fool, especially considering the news she was about to break.

But when all was said and done, she should come out the

winner. She was convinced Jake was innocent, and she'd lose some of her hard-earned credibility if she announced his guilt to the city and was proven wrong.

The news anchor appeared on the monitor, and Lisa held her breath when he announced her story. A full-length shot of her came on the screen, with the Richmond Hill General Hospital sign prominently displayed in the background as she spoke:

"Citizens of Richmond Hill were shocked earlier this week at my announcement of the shooting of Merrilla Overstone. My investigation revealed Overstone was a loan manager at the Commerce Bank, the financial institution robbed a day prior to her shooting.

"After I revealed the undeniable link between the two events, police explored the situation further. Though the suspect wanted for both the robbery of Commerce Bank and the shooting of Mrs. Overstone is yet to be named, I'm assured an arrest is imminent. Reliable sources tell me a manhunt is underway and has been for the last thirty-six hours.

"Since the shooting on Tuesday, Mrs. Overstone has remained in intensive care, kept under close watch. Police had hoped her testimony would bring an end to this unfortunate situation, resulting in the arrest of any third party who might've been involved in, or have knowledge of, either crime.

"However, it now appears the situation has become further complicated. I've been told that within the last hour, Merrilla Overstone has succumbed to her injury. She passed away quietly

without further comments that might aid police in their hunt for the perpetrator.

"I spoke to Niles Overstone earlier today, when Merrilla's husband expressed support for his wife. At that time, he had announced she'd been diagnosed with pancreatic cancer a year ago and may now have as little as a few weeks to live. Whether or not her illness contributed to her unfortunate death is unknown at this time.

"In light of the passing of Merrilla Overstone, I've decided it would be best to air the interview with a minimum of editing."

Lisa turned away from the monitor. She'd heard Niles Overstone's story once too often already, and she hoped it wasn't too boring for her listeners. She'd heavily edited the interview, taking out the worst parts—the segments where Overstone had droned on and on ad nauseam about his wife's virtues and how much they loved each other.

After editing, what remained of the lengthy interview would be sufficient to give the best impact. It would be sure to coax out a few tears from among a certain segment of her audience. That was always good for ratings.

But what bothered her the most was, now that Mrs. Overstone had died, the police would no doubt intensify their hunt for Jake. She feared they would announce his name to the public, and her deal with the Lincolns would vanish.

And though she found it hard to admit, she did owe the Lincolns a big favor. If she could find a way to get to the bottom of this and help Jake out, that would repay what she owed them and secure her deal at the same time.

She'd have to give it some thought, and she would undoubtedly come up with an idea she could run with bright and early in the morning.

~*~

ANNIE TURNED OFF the television and sat back, surprised and disturbed at the announcement of Merrilla Overstone's death. She'd hoped the woman would recover well enough to speak coherently, possibly for long enough to identify her real shooter.

Things were looking worse and worse for Jake.

And for her.

The last part of the story had contained video of the bank robbery, with the footage of the actual shooting removed. At least Lisa had kept her word and not mentioned Jake's name. No doubt convinced of his innocence, she'd urged members of the public to contact her or the police if they recognized the suspect.

Matty had been asking about his father again, and Annie was finding it hard to skirt around the truth. And it looked like there was going to be at least one more night without Jake's presence.

She sighed and went into the kitchen for her cell phone, then sat at the table nursing a cup of coffee and dialed Jake's number.

"I'm on the streets," Jake said. "I have a lead. I'm looking for a guy named Dewey Hicks. He might be behind this whole thing." She listened with hope in her heart as he filled her in on the events of the afternoon. "He's a night owl. I might have to wait until a little later to track him down."

That was good news, and Annie hoped the information Jake would be sure to get would clear his name and bring him home to his family.

"I wonder if I should call Hank," Annie said. "He might be able to get me something on Hicks."

"I'm sure Hank'll discover the guy has a record a mile long," Jake said. "But right now, it's only a name. It doesn't prove anything. I'm pretty sure I can track him down without Hank's help. Once I do, I'll find out what's going on. If I get something solid, I'll let you know. Then you can talk to Hank."

"I'll put it off until tomorrow, but we have another problem," Annie said. "Lisa just announced on the news that Merrilla Overstone died less than an hour ago."

Jake took a sharp breath and remained quiet.

"That means you're wanted for two murders now," Annie said. "Two murders you didn't commit."

"And my best witness is dead. That sure throws a wrench into things."

Annie told Jake about her afternoon excursion, and about the keys she'd discovered and what she had done with them. "I don't like breaking the law," she said. "But I had to do something."

"I guess I'm breaking a few laws myself," Jake said. "But it seems like it's the only way to get anything done. We're in this thing alone."

"Speaking of being alone, where're you going to sleep tonight?"

Jake chuckled. "I haven't decided yet. The cops are bound to be all over this now that Merrilla's dead, and I've no idea what Hank might do. I can't go back to Sammy's place." He paused. "But don't worry. I'll find someplace nice and warm to curl up."

"I hope the safe deposit box keys lead somewhere," Annie said. "I'll talk to Hank tomorrow and see if I can get something out of him without mentioning anything specific."

"Knowing Hank, he'll get around to mentioning the keys. He's gonna know they're from you."

"Doesn't matter. He won't pursue it. He's got enough to handle right now."

"I'd better go," Jake said. "My charge is getting low, and I don't know where to charge it up again."

"You still have money left?"

"Lots of money. At least a couple hundred. As long as I don't have to pay too many people off, I'll be okay."

"Let me know if you find Hicks, and I'll talk to you soon," Annie said, then hung up the phone.

Finally, things were starting to happen, but she didn't know how much longer either of them could hold out. Some of her regular clients had contacted her regarding research and background checks that couldn't wait. She'd put off returning their calls; her heart wasn't in it right now.

As long as she had nothing else pressing to do, she'd call them back first thing in the morning. A bit of mundane research might be what she needed to take her mind off her current predicament.

Until she came up with another idea, she'd have to leave their future up to Jake.

CHAPTER 29

Wednesday, 8:44 p.m.

FOR THE THIRD TIME in the last two hours, Jake pulled open the pitted wooden door of Gully's Bar and stepped into the smoke-filled room. The last time he'd wandered in and looked around, the bartender had given him a curious glance before turning back to serve a customer. The same bartender now paused his task of polishing the drab bar and turned his eyes toward Jake.

If the proprietor's piercing look was any indication, perhaps the two punks weren't the only ones who thought Jake was a cop. With two full days' growth of beard on his face, and his short-cropped hair, he probably looked like a cop trying too hard not to look like a cop.

Jake went to the bar and climbed onto a stool, spinning it around to face the dimly lit room. The barroom was filling up with noisy customers. Half of the tables were occupied by groups of two or three. The rest of the patrons hung around pool tables or lounged on barstools to his right and left.

Dewey Hicks could very well be among them. The problem was, Jake had no way of knowing what the guy looked like.

The two hoods he'd questioned had said Hicks hung around here a lot. That meant he should be known by any other punks who happened to frequent this seedy establishment. And drinkers were arriving in droves. Jake decided that this time, he was gonna hang around as long as was necessary. But he'd have to buy a drink to keep the bartender from eyeing him.

"What can I get for you?"

Jake spun his stool to face the bartender. "Draft."

The guy nodded and left without a word.

Jake peeled a ten-dollar bill from his dwindling stash, laid it on the bar, and waited for the bartender to return.

"Want change?"

Jake shook his head. "Keep the change. By the way, I'm looking for Dewey Hicks. You seen him around yet?"

The bartender frowned and folded the ten, dropping it into his shirt pocket. "Don't know no Hicks."

"You sure? I'm supposed to meet him here. Got a package for him from Mikey."

The man's frown deepened. "Don't know no Mikey, either."

Jake decided he probably did look like a cop.

He shrugged and took a small sip of beer. From the corner of his eye, he watched the bartender move away to look after another customer.

Sliding his beer over with him, Jake moved to the next stool. He kept his head down and his eyes up, training them on a grimy mirror that backed a long row of spirits behind the bar. Through the mirror, he had almost a full view of the entire room.

Customers came and went, and Jake waited.

A few minutes later, the bartender looked around, probably checking to see if anyone needed his immediate attention, then wiped his hands on his jeans and slipped out from behind the bar. He moved toward the back of the room and stopped beside a couple of guys who lounged at a small round table.

The bartender leaned over and his lips moved. The slimy-looking guy he was addressing glanced toward the bar and gave a slight nod. Then, tilting his chair back on two legs, the guy dropped a foot on a chair beside him and crossed his arms. Jake felt curious eyes on his back as he watched the punk through the mirror.

The bartender returned and served up some drinks to thirsty patrons, then leaned against a cabinet and yawned.

Pushing back his beer, Jake slipped off the barstool and stood. In his peripheral vision, he saw the guy he hoped was Hicks drop his foot to the floor and sit forward. His eyes followed as Jake ambled toward the door and pulled it open.

Jake stepped from the bar and headed across the street. He reached the sidewalk on the other side and turned his head, taking an indifferent glance toward the bar. The punk and two of his friends stood on the sidewalk, watching him. Jake stuffed his hands into his pockets and strolled casually up the street.

He hoped the punks were following him. A glance into the window of a storefront assured him they were.

Half a block later, Jake turned into an alley. He'd checked out the entire area earlier, and he knew the alley was a dead end, stopping a hundred feet ahead at a high wooden fence. He was betting the punks knew it, too. The only exit from the darkened lane was either through one of the doors on either side, or back the way he'd come.

Jake reached the end of the alley and made a pretense of trying to work his way over the fence, then appeared to give up and turn back.

The three punks were heading down the alley, one in front, the other two close behind.

They stopped. "I hear you're looking for me," the one in front said, crossing his arms.

Jake stopped five feet away. "You Hicks?"

"Who wants to know?"

Jake stepped closer and held out his hand. "Mikey sent me."

Hicks looked curiously at the outstretched hand, then glared at Jake. "Who's Mikey?"

Without warning, Jake's hand shot up, and his fingers wrapped around Hicks's throat and squeezed. His free hand was clenched into a fist and ready as the other two punks moved in. He caught the closest one full in the face, and the startled man went down onto his back, holding his bruised nose and howling in pain.

The other guy paused midstride, then turned and beat a path out of the alley faster than Jake had ever seen anyone run. The guy probably figured he'd sooner deal with a betrayed Hicks later rather than taking a chance against Jake's massive fist and ending up like his partner.

Hicks cursed between gasping breaths, struggling with both hands to free himself from Jake's grasp, but Jake held on.

The guy on the ground groaned again, then rolled to unsteady feet and stumbled away, his hands nursing his bruised and bleeding face.

"What … what d'you want?" Hicks managed to spit out between curse words and shallow breaths.

Jake turned around and dragged an angry Hicks with him, trapping the punk between himself and the fence.

Hicks backed up and thumped against the wooden barrier. He didn't look so tough now, and he cowered in fear as Jake moved in and towered over him.

"I didn't do nothin' to you."

Jake leaned in, his face inches from the trembling man. "You set me up."

"I don't even know who you are."

Jake sighed. "You have a choice."

Hicks looked confused. "What choice?"

"Which arm do you want me to break first?"

Hicks looked frantically towards the only path to escape, then looked up at Jake and remained quiet.

Jake grabbed Hicks by his right arm. "We'll do this one first and leave the other one for later."

"Wait. You don't wanna do that."

Jake shrugged and tightened his grip. "You're right. I really don't, but I guess I have to. It'll make me feel bad for a while, but I'll get over it."

"I ... I mean, you don't hafta do that. What d'you wanna know?"

"I want to know about the bank robbery. Who robbed the Commerce Bank?"

"Wasn't me."

"I know it wasn't you," Jake said. "You're just a measly little punk, and you're gonna tell me who did."

Hicks bit his lip and looked frantically around.

Jake twisted the arm, and Hicks howled. "All right. I'll tell you."

"Who robbed the bank?"

Hicks paused, looked at Jake's bulging biceps, then said in a low voice, "It was Ace."

"Ace who?"

"Don't know. Just Ace."

"Where can I find this Ace character?"

Hicks shook his head. "I don't see him around much. Haven't seen him since yesterday morning. He lives north, near the bank. That's all I know."

"What's he look like?"

"He looks a bit like you. Big. Muscles all over the place."

Jake dropped Hicks's arm and moved back a step. "Tell me about Merrilla Overstone."

Hicks looked genuinely confused. "Don't know nobody named Overstone."

Jake leaned in and scowled. "The woman who was shot."

Hicks's expression didn't change.

"You know me, don't you?" Jake asked.

Hicks gave a weak nod.

"You set me up. You planted the money in my garage."

The punk's eyes told Jake he had.

"Ace paid you to plant the money?"

Another nod.

As long as Hicks wasn't feeding him a line, it appeared Ace had been the one who had shot Merrilla Overstone, then had hired Hicks to help with the frame job.

Jake straightened up and crossed his arms. "You might see me around again. And if you do, you'd better know where I can find Ace."

"I … I'll see what I can do."

"You don't want your arms broken, am I right?"

Hicks nodded vigorously.

Jake stepped aside. "You can go now, but remember, I'm watching you."

Hicks scurried past Jake and raced from the alley.

Jake watched him go, sure that Hicks would be having a nasty talk with his two friends before long. But they were all punks, and Jake still had to find one more punk—a guy named Ace.

CHAPTER 30

NILES OVERSTONE awoke with a sudden start and sat up in bed. Though he was dead tired, he hadn't been sleeping soundly the last two nights, and the faint sound of someone moving around had brought him out of his shallow sleep.

The morning sun was streaming through his window, lighting up his bedroom. At first he thought Merrilla was awake and getting dressed quietly like she always did, doing her best to let him sleep for another half hour.

Then the awful reality hit him again. Merrilla wasn't coming home. The last few weeks they'd planned together had vanished. He lay back and closed his eyes, squeezing away fresh tears.

After the death of his wife, the police had unsealed his house and allowed him to return. At first he hadn't wanted to, but he and his wife had talked about this at length a few weeks ago. Merrilla's wishes had been that he stay in their house, and she'd persisted until he made her that promise. Her imminent death had been a tough subject to discuss, but once they'd both come to accept the inevitable, it was one of the things his wife had been determined about.

The doorknob rattled and he sprang to a sitting position. His instinct had been correct. Someone was out there, and it wasn't Merrilla, and they didn't belong in his house.

He leaped out of bed, fully awake now, and glanced at the window. Whoever was coming into his bedroom would be inside in a matter of seconds, and it would take him a lot longer than that to get the window open and climb outside.

Racing across the carpeted floor to the open double-width closet, he dove inside and cowered back against the wall, hidden behind a row of clothes his wife would never need again.

The bedroom door squeaked, and he held his breath, his heart pounding in his chest. He heard muffled breathing, then a grunt and a curse as the intruder no doubt had discovered the empty bed.

His thoughts raced at high speed. It had to be Jake Lincoln coming to finish the job. For the same reason Lincoln had killed his beloved wife, whatever that reason was, he had now come to kill him as well.

Then footsteps sounded on a tile floor; the killer had gone to the master bathroom. He heard the faint sound of the shower door opening, and he had but a moment to spare.

Niles sprang from the closet, brushing two or three

dresses off the rod in his haste to escape. Wire hangers rattled together as they hit the floor, and for a moment, his feet became tangled in his wife's precious belongings he'd so carelessly knocked from their perch.

Kicking the clothes free, he dove for the open doorway leading into the upstairs hallway. The intruder shouted something he didn't understand, and as his bare feet hit the slick wooden floor of the hall, Niles slipped and landed on his hip, causing him to cry out in pain.

The fall might've saved him, at least for the time being. A bullet whistled through the space his head had occupied a moment earlier. A window shattered at the end of the hallway as the projectile burst through the glass and continued on.

He rolled once, twice, his head smashing against the solid base of the oak banister leading down to the main level of the house. It stunned him for a second, and he caught a brief glimpse of the shooter, now in the process of swinging his gun hand toward him.

His assailant's head nearly touched the top of the doorframe as he lined his weapon up for another shot. It was Jake Lincoln. The man's face was hidden in shadows, but the heavily muscled arms and the broad shoulders were a dead giveaway.

Rolling again, Niles tumbled down half a dozen steps, his soft pajama bottoms gaining no traction on the polished wooden stairs. Then, with the aid of the railing, he managed to come upright. He staggered downward and leaped the last three steps, his naked feet slapping against the hardwood floor at the bottom of the stairs.

The killer's shoes pounded on the steps above him, and the weapon exploded again. Somewhere behind him, Niles heard the zing of the bullet as he dashed for the kitchen.

He tripped on a rug at the entrance to the room and fell forward, gliding across the ceramic floor. His head came to rest against the back door that led to the yard outside and his best chance of escape.

He scrambled to his feet, then realized he'd never make it out. He was directly between the door and the shooter. A third shot would be sure to finish him before he could manage to remove the chain, unlock the door, and get outside.

For a brief moment, he considered giving up. That would be the easiest way out of the dreadful mess life had thrown at him. He could join his wife in a better place, where his emotional turmoil would vanish. He had nothing to live for now, anyway.

His better judgment took over, and he glanced around in desperation.

He had left his cell phone in the bedroom, not thinking of anything but escape at the time. He looked at the landline on the kitchen wall. There was no chance to make a call, and there was no one who could help him in time. He was on his own.

The killer's hurried footsteps drew closer. How could Niles possibly protect himself from a murderer with a loaded weapon?

He couldn't, and his only chance to live would be to run

or to hide. But there was no place to hide in the kitchen. He'd have to run.

He leaped across the island, hit the floor on the other side, and raced for the adjoining living room. It circled around to the kitchen again, and the shooter could bide his time and come at him from either direction.

The front door of the house was securely locked. He wasn't about to spend his last precious moments fumbling with the lock, only to be shot down like a dog and left to die alone in his own blood.

Niles dove out of sight behind an easy chair and came to a crouch, closing his eyes in an attempt to still the panic. His rasping breath sounded like thunder. His heart raced. His mind spun furiously, hoping to come up with a way out of his desperate situation.

But there was no way out.

The gunman's footsteps sounded in the kitchen, then the soft squeal of leather on wood as they came closer. The awful sound stopped, and the killer breathed, in and out, in and out, and Niles held his breath and prayed.

He knew Lincoln had been here before and probably knew every entrance and exit. But Niles had taken precautions to double-lock every door and make sure all the windows were fastened.

From where Niles crouched, he could see the door leading to the basement. It was closed. If the shooter had entered the house through a basement window, he surely would've left the door open to make a fast exit.

The kitchen window had been closed, the back door

securely locked. The bathroom window was barely large enough for a child to crawl through, let alone a man of Lincoln's size.

That left only two possible means of entrance—the office and the spare bedroom.

The office faced the front of the house—not exactly a stealthy means of entrance, especially during early daylight hours.

Lincoln had to have entered through the window of the spare bedroom.

If Niles stayed where he was, he'd surely die. If he tried his dangerous and desperate plan, he might live.

There was no choice.

He braced himself, tensing his leg muscles, then took a deep breath and shot to his feet, springing out from behind his only protection.

The shooter whirled and swung his weapon toward the sudden movement.

Niles would have but a split second to spare. Any longer, and he might feel the stinging bite of a bullet in his back, bringing him down and dying at the murderer's feet.

He spun down the short hallway, now momentarily out of the view of the gunman, desperately hoping his analysis of the mind of the killer had been correct.

Otherwise, he was as good as dead.

Without slowing, he dashed through the open door of the spare bedroom and leaped.

Straight through the open window.

He hit the ground hard, bruising a shoulder, then

stumbled to his feet as another bullet zipped past his head.

Two seconds later, Niles had reached the sidewalk. He looked back over his shoulder as he raced up the street. The killer had retreated.

He was bruised and frightened half to death, but he was going to live.

CHAPTER 31

Thursday, 7:32 a.m.

HANK SAT AT THE kitchen table in his apartment, sipping at his second cup of coffee, when his cell phone rang. Niles Overstone had been accosted in his home by a would-be killer but had managed to escape, calling 9-1-1 from a neighbor's house. Hank was needed at once.

The news was disturbing. They'd allowed the distraught man to return home after the death of his wife, only to have his house broken into and his life threatened. And to make matters worse for Overstone, his house would be sealed up again. And this time, no doubt entry would be barred until the case had been cleaned up.

The entire block would be canvassed in the hopes someone might've seen something or someone suspicious in the area. It was unusual a crime of this nature would've taken place at that time of day, but with this case, anything was possible.

CSI would still be at the crime scene, and Hank looked forward to their report. He'd take a walk through the scene later, but first, he wanted to talk to Overstone.

Hank looked at his watch. The timing was perfect. He was about to head to work in a few minutes, anyway.

He dumped his half-finished coffee into the sink along with his breakfast dishes, then strapped on his service weapon, grabbed his briefcase, and left the apartment.

On his way to the precinct, he thought about what this new development meant to his theory. Though there'd been no evidence of Overstone's involvement in the shooting of his wife, he'd still remained a viable suspect, perhaps connected to it in some way yet unknown.

But now that the man's life had been threatened, what did that mean?

Had the murderer of Merrilla Overstone returned to kill Niles? Or was the man involved somehow, and there was another reason for the attempt on his life?

Or a more disturbing possibility was that the alleged attempted murder was a cock-and-bull story created by Overstone to throw suspicion away from himself. There were no known witnesses to the invasion, and perhaps there was no one out to get him at all.

Hank was also disturbed the information regarding Merrilla's cancer hadn't been shared with him earlier. Though the surgeon had later confirmed it was not a contributing factor to her death, it was a small piece of information he'd like to have had.

When Hank arrived at the precinct, he approached Yappy,

sitting at reception. He was informed Overstone was in interview room one with an officer. The man was in the process of filling out a written statement.

He was surprised to see Detective King at his desk. His partner would also have received a call notifying him of the attempted murder, and though King still looked half-asleep, at least he'd made the attempt to get here without delay.

He went to King's desk and dropped into a chair. "What do you make of the shooting?"

King tossed the papers he was browsing onto the desk and sat back. "Dunno. I thought Overstone hired a hitman to kill his wife." He shrugged. "Now I don't know what's going on."

"Package for you, Hank." The voice came from Yappy, and he approached the desk and handed Hank an envelope personally addressed to him at RHPD.

"Thanks, Yappy," Hank said. He turned the envelope over in his hands, then borrowed King's letter opener and slit it open. He pulled out a small brown package and peered inside, then dumped a pair of keys onto the desk and frowned at them.

"Safe deposit box keys," King said. "Who's it from?"

"No return address."

"Nothing else inside?"

"Nope." Hank leaned in and squinted at one of the keys, then pointed. "There's the Commerce Bank logo."

"Commerce Bank," King said. "That's the bank that was robbed."

"Yup."

"And that's where Merrilla Overstone worked."

"It sure is, and I'm betting these keys will fit nicely into one of the boxes from that branch."

King tilted his chair back and dropped his feet onto the edge of the desk, crossing them at the ankles. "Wonder what's inside."

"Why don't you go and find out? You should be able to obtain a warrant by telephone." Hank dropped the keys back into the envelope and tossed the package to his partner.

King dropped the keys into his shirt pocket, then stood and turned to leave.

"Get back as fast as you can," Hank said. "It might be important."

"Will do."

Hank took his briefcase to his desk and set it beside his chair. He needed to talk to Overstone personally, but he would give the man half an hour to finish with his statement, and if King was back by then, so much the better.

Half an hour later, King still hadn't returned. Hank decided to start the interview without his partner and see where it led.

He went to interview room one and stepped inside the open door. An officer greeted him, handed him a folder, then left the room.

Niles Overstone was leaning forward at the metal table with his head down, his elbows on the table, and his face in his hands.

Hank dropped the folder onto the desk, then pulled back a chair opposite the man and sat down.

Niles lowered his hands. His once-youthful face looked haggard and old. Visible tear tracks ran down his face. He wiped the moisture away with the palm of his hand and looked at Hank through bloodshot eyes.

If Overstone was faking his grief, he was doing a good job.

"Mr. Overstone," Hank began, observing the man as he spoke. "I'm very sorry to hear about your wife."

Overstone gave a slight nod.

"I realize this is hard for you, but I have to ask you a few questions."

Another nod.

"First, did you happen to get a glimpse of the man who shot you?"

Overstone's eyes narrowed. "It was Jake Lincoln."

Hank wasn't expecting to hear that. He was becoming more and more convinced of Jake's innocence.

He leaned forward and laid his arms on the table. "Are you sure? Did you see his face?"

"It was him."

"Are you saying you saw his face clearly?"

Niles shook his head. "No. I didn't see his face."

"Then how can you be sure?"

"By his size. His build. It had to be him. He killed my wife. Who else could it be?"

Hank sat back. "That's a good question." He felt a small amount of relief Overstone couldn't positively identify Jake, but nonetheless, the news was disturbing. There was no point in asking the man who else might be out to get him. He was already convinced it was Jake.

He opened the folder and scanned Overstone's statement. Though the handwritten information went into detail, taking up two full pages, he didn't see a mention of Jake's name.

Hank closed the folder and looked at Overstone. "You obviously can't go home right away," he said. "Do you have a place to stay?"

"I think I'll go back to Richmond Inn for now. Wanda, my wife's sister, offered to put me up. She's been a big help to me lately, but I'd sooner be alone right now." He paused and his eyes glazed over. "My ... wife's body was released last night, and Wanda started funeral arrangements immediately."

Hank knew since the victim had died in the hospital under a doctor's care, there was no necessity for an autopsy. If the cause of death was clear, the body would be released.

"I talked to Wanda a while ago," Overstone continued. "There'll be a wake this evening, and the ... funeral is tomorrow."

Hank would be sure to arrange for a police presence at both events. Whoever had tried to kill Niles Overstone might return at the most unexpected moment and, as well as safeguarding Overstone, Hank wanted to be ready for anything.

The door of the interview room swung open and King stood outside. He beckoned toward Hank.

"What do you have?" Hank asked in a hushed voice after he'd stepped from the room.

King handed Hank a thick envelope. "It's a life insurance policy on Merrilla Overstone. Three million bucks. Made out to Niles Overstone."

Hank's eyes widened, then narrowed again. "How'd we not know about this before?"

"The box and the policy are both in Merrilla's maiden name."

"Is the policy up to date?"

"It sure is."

"That opens a whole new can of worms," Hank said. He opened the package and glanced briefly at its contents. "It's good, all right. The policy was first made out years ago, long before Merrilla was diagnosed with cancer."

"It makes a great motive for murder," King said. "But why was it in a safe deposit box?"

"Let's find out."

Hank led the way back into the interview room, laid the policy on the table, and slid it toward Overstone. "What can you tell me about this?"

Overstone picked up the papers, and his eyes shot open a few moments later. "I had no idea."

"None?"

Niles sat the policy back down and pushed it away. "I'd sooner have my wife than … this."

King leaned in, about to say something, but Hank stopped him with a look. His partner straightened up and leaned against the wall, frowning at Overstone.

"I went through my wife's things yesterday," Overstone said. "Where did you find it?"

"It was in a safe deposit box at the bank where she worked."

Niles looked bewildered, then he dropped his head and

spoke. "That's why Merrilla was so at peace about dying. She knew I'd be taken care of financially."

"Unless you had her killed," King said. "Then it's void."

Overstone shot King a look of disgust, then glared at Hank. "You don't think I had anything to do with this, do you?"

"We have to look into all possibilities," Hank said. "In the meantime, you're free to go anytime you want."

Overstone stared darkly a moment and then stood. "I'll be at Richmond Inn if you need me." Then he brushed past King and strode from the room.

King shrugged and followed, leaving Hank wondering if Overstone knew more than he was saying. Three million dollars would go a long way toward buying the new widower a life of ease.

CHAPTER 32

Thursday, 9:33 a.m.

AFTER JAKE'S LITTLE talk with Hicks the evening before, he'd spent the next couple of hours patrolling the bars and other seedy establishments throughout the neighborhood. He'd asked a few questions, but mostly, he'd watched and listened. In places where everyone seemed to know everyone else, he was the outsider, receiving the silent treatment and drawing curious stares.

After a short talk with Sammy, the homeless man had recommended a secluded spot where he could catch some sleep. Jake had been dog-tired, and he'd finally slipped into the rear of an abandoned building and lay down for what was left of the night.

The streets were quiet now, with only a few hard-working and honest citizens treading the narrow sidewalks. The unsavory side of the area's inhabitants would likely sleep until noon, then wander out and eventually congregate at their usual haunts for the late-evening hours.

And somewhere among them was a man named Ace—the key to solving Jake's problem. Finding him wasn't going to be an easy task.

But right now, his stomach was asking for food. The only restaurant in the area less grimy than the rest was a little dump where he was now headed. He'd been there before, and the place was usually packed at breakfast time. It must have something going for it.

A bell jingled when Jake pulled opened the grubby door. He stepped inside and was greeted by the smell of frying bacon. Finding an empty booth near the back of the room, he sat and brushed the last patron's toast crumbs off the table, then looked around.

Years of built-up grease and grime covered the walls, the floor much the same. At least the lighting was sufficient, and Jake would be able to see what he was eating.

On the far side of a narrow counter lined with stools and hungry customers, the cook expertly flipped some sputtering eggs onto a plate, then spun around and slipped it onto the counter behind him. The establishment's only waitress swooped up the plate, delivering the meal and a refreshing smile to a waiting customer two booths away.

Jake ordered the king-sized breakfast from the friendly waitress and waited.

The bell on the door jingled again, and Jake looked toward the sound. He slouched down and pulled his hat low when two men stepped into the restaurant.

They were cops.

Jake recognized the two narcos. He'd seen them around the precinct, and like most of the cops there, he knew their names and had talked to them several times in the past.

And they knew him.

Detective Benson was the biggest of the pair. Almost as large as Jake, the cop spent a lot of time undercover, busting drug dealers and drug lords. With his cold beady eyes and whiskered face, he could easily be mistaken for one of the many lowlifes who hung around the neighborhood.

The other guy was Detective O'Day, and he was as Irish as his name. Not more than five foot seven, the beefy cop's arrogant demeanor said he wasn't a guy you wanted to get on the wrong side of.

The truth was, they were a couple of the nicest guys Jake had ever talked with. According to Hank, the pair were incorruptible. Tough when they needed to be, their looks served them well, and they fit comfortably into their undercover roles.

But their presence was a threat.

When they slid into a booth three tables away, Jake kept his head low and slipped over a few inches, now out of Benson's view behind O'Day's meaty head.

The restaurant was a dangerous place to be right now, and Jake weighed his options. He could keep his head turned, then work his way to the front door and make tracks out of there. Or perhaps he could wait it out. But that was risky, too.

The third option was the most sensible. These joints always had a back door, and that was the way out of his dicey situation.

His meal would have to wait.

He dropped a ten-dollar bill on the table and raised his head. His eyes met Benson's, and for a moment, both men froze.

Then the cop's mouth fell open and his eyes enlarged, and Jake didn't wait around.

"Lincoln! Stop!" It was Benson shouting from behind Jake, who was now halfway toward the back of the room.

A hand-painted arrow on the wall pointed to the bathrooms downstairs. A door led off to his right, another one dead ahead, and for a valuable split second, Jake paused.

"Lincoln!"

Jake took the door ahead of him and dashed into a storage room. Directly ahead, an exit sign hung above another door. Jake dove forward and rammed against the push bar, and the door swung open.

He raced into an access lane and looked at his surroundings. An overloaded dumpster sat to the right. A rat skittered away, frightened out of his meal. Further down, the lane led to a side street.

Ahead he faced a brick wall, and to his left, the alley ended at a ten-foot chain-link fence.

He went left, electing to outmaneuver his pursuers rather than outrun them.

The door crashed open behind him.

Jake whipped down the alley, then, three feet short of the fence, his powerful leg muscles vaulted him upwards. His fingers clung to the wire a foot short of the top, and his feet struggled to gain some footing.

"Lincoln. We have to talk."

Jake got one hand on the top and, with the help of his feet, managed to work himself up. He did a handstand, then dropped to his feet on the other side.

"Jake. Wait."

Jake glanced toward the voice. Benson had stopped short of the fence, O'Day coming to a standstill beside him.

Benson held out one hand, palm out, and O'Day crossed his arms and frowned.

Unless one of the cops pulled a weapon, they were no longer an immediate threat. He'd be long gone before either one of them could make it over the high barrier.

Jake moved closer to the fence, crossed his arms, and looked at the detectives through the wire.

"Jake, you should surrender," O'Day said.

"I can't. I didn't do what they say I did, and I'm the only one who can prove it."

Benson took a step closer and faced Jake through the fence, his small, steady eyes burrowing into Jake's. He stared and breathed, then finally spoke in a soft voice. "O'Day and I don't think you're guilty, either, Jake. But we're cops. Our hands are tied."

"Not if you didn't see me," Jake said.

O'Day moved up beside Benson and looked at his partner, his frown now replaced by a confused look. "Who're you talking to? I don't see anybody."

Benson chuckled.

"Look, guys," Jake said, "I had a little conversation with a punk named Dewey Hicks—"

"Hicks?" Benson interrupted. "You're right about Hicks being a punk, but he's not smooth enough to pull this off."

"No, he sure isn't," Jake said. "But he told me a guy named Ace was behind this whole thing. And Ace hired Hicks to plant the evidence in my garage."

O'Day shook his head, pursing his lips. "Never heard of Ace."

"Hicks said Ace isn't from around here."

Benson spoke. "And this Ace guy is the one you're looking for?"

"I hope it's him," Jake said. "I don't think Hicks was trying to pull a fast one."

O'Day laughed. "That depends on how nicely you asked him."

"Only as nice as I needed to be."

"Hicks is a coward. I'm betting it's the truth."

"Then, I have to find Ace," Jake said.

Benson glanced at O'Day, then back at Jake. "We can ask around, but it's not really in our field of expertise. Unless he's a druggie, we might not have any luck."

"I don't know exactly what he's into," Jake said. "But I'm pretty sure he killed two people."

"How can we contact you?" O'Day said.

Jake hesitated. The cops seemed like they were on the up and up, and he was pretty sure they wouldn't go out of their way to track him down after this. Nevertheless, he couldn't take that chance.

"You can contact Annie if you find out anything," Jake said. "But if you come across any ironclad proof, talk to Hank."

Benson breathed out a long breath, almost like a groan. "You're putting us on the spot, Jake. It's not our case, and if we go breaking a few arms and asking questions on behalf of a fugitive—"

"You won't be sorry."

O'Day looked at Benson and shrugged. "What's the harm in giving him a break? Especially since it's all a setup. Besides, we never saw him, and our breakfast is getting cold."

Benson pointed a finger at Jake. "You'd better get out of here before you land us all in jail."

"I'm gone," Jake said. "Thanks, guys."

Benson and O'Day disappeared inside the building, and Jake turned away.

Once this was cleared up, he'd have to remember he owed them a favor.

CHAPTER 33

Thursday, 11:00 a.m.

ANNIE HAD FOUND IT impossible to concentrate on anything but thoughts of her husband. She'd spent another sleepless night, the second without Jake beside her. Her dreams had been filled with horrible visions of her and Jake chained in a dungeon, with no possibility of escape, while Hank lounged outside their cell and laughed uncontrollably.

The morning light had washed those nightmares away, and after seeing Matty off to school, she'd spent most of the morning at her desk, going over her growing file of evidence.

Jake had called her late last night, and today she'd been digging for information on a man called Ace. It was futile. There were too many guys who went by the name of Ace, nothing more than a nickname designed to impress the easily impressed.

After all the time she'd spent agonizing over every note, every report, and every scrap of paper in the folder, there still didn't seem to be any clear answer to the largest problem they'd ever faced.

When her cell phone rang, and Hank's number appeared on the caller ID, she answered it, hoping he had some good news for her. Instead, what she received was a gentle scolding.

"Annie, I appreciate that your life has been turned upside down, but please, let me do my job. Do what you have to, but do it legally."

Annie took a deep breath. "Whatever are you talking about, Hank?"

"I think you know."

She knew, all right. But of course, she couldn't admit anything. Not to a cop, even if he was a close friend.

"Did you find anything?" she asked.

Hank chuckled. "Other than what I found in my mail this morning, yes, I did."

Annie waited for Hank to continue. He didn't, and she was getting impatient. "What did you find, Hank?"

"A motive."

"A motive? For who?"

"Niles Overstone."

Hank was taking his sweet time getting to the point. He was either not going to tell her, or he was punishing her in some small way for her illegal transgression.

Annie sighed. "Hank, if you ever want to be invited to this house again for a home-cooked meal, you'd better spit it out."

"Are you bribing a cop?"

"Absolutely."

Hank laughed out loud. "Then I'd better tell you. We found a life insurance policy for three million dollars on Merrilla Overstone, payable to her husband."

"And it's good?"

"It's good."

Annie let out a whistling breath. "That's a great motive," she said, then added, "But it doesn't clear Jake."

"Nope. And it also doesn't implicate anyone else. It's not proof of any wrongdoing. Just a possible motive."

Annie had hoped something more earth-shattering would've been found in the box. Though it was a minor letdown, the information seemed to be swaying Hank's way of thinking. And if it eased the pressure off Jake, allowing him to move about more freely, it was a good thing.

"Hank, there's something else I need to talk to you about. When Jake told you he'd taken pictures of the intruder at the Overstone house, he wouldn't lie about that. Why would he? It would be one of the dumbest things he ever did. I'm sure someone deleted them. And I'm sure it was the same person who planted the burner phone under the seat of the car."

"You can't prove a negative," Hank said. "Absence of evidence is not evidence of absence."

"Quit with the philosophical stuff and listen," Annie said. "I happen to know anything deleted off a hard drive is not deleted. Only the catalog information that points to the files is gone. As long as nothing else is written to the drive in the meantime, the files aren't overwritten. They can be recovered. Wouldn't the same hold true for a flash drive?"

Hank was quiet a moment, then said, "Sounds reasonable, but I don't pretend to be an expert. I can run it past Callaway. He's not in today, and there's no one else who can do what he does. But I'll get him to take a look at it first thing tomorrow morning."

"And if it works out, Hank, I hope you'll seriously consider Jake's story."

Hank sighed. "Annie, my dear friend, I do seriously consider Jake's story. It's the lack of proof I have a problem with. I have nothing to back up what Jake said happened, and I can only go with what the evidence shows. I wish I could call off the dogs, but I can't. But rest assured, most of them aren't actively pursuing the hunt for Jake."

"Then recover that drive, and have a good look at that insurance policy. And there's one more thing. I've heard from a reliable source a man named Ace is neck-deep in this."

"Any last name?"

"No. Just Ace."

"Did your reliable source tell you where I could find this Ace fellow?"

"No, but I was hoping you could do some digging and come up with something. It's a dead end for me."

"There's nothing much I can do without a last name, Annie. I'll take a look at it, and I'll run the name past the other guys, but tell your reliable source to be careful out there. If Ace is a killer, he'll kill again to protect himself from being found out."

"I'll tell him," Annie said.

"Is there anything else?"

"Not right now."

"Then let me get back to work on this," Hank said, then he was gone.

Annie hung up the phone thoughtfully. Progress was slow, but it seemed they might be getting somewhere at last. And if Jake could stay out of danger, and the police didn't nab him, she was confident everything would work out in the end. Whenever that was.

She was startled when the phone on her desk rang, and this time it was an unknown number.

"Lincoln Investigations."

"Is this Annie?"

"Yes."

"Annie, this is Detective Benson. My partner, Detective O'Day, and I, uh ... had occasion to hear that Jake's looking for a guy named Ace."

Annie sat forward. She knew Benson and O'Day quite well, and she knew Jake did, too. "Nice to hear from you, Detective. Did you find out who and where this Ace character is?"

"First of all, Annie, this call's strictly confidential. I'm calling you against my better judgment."

"You couldn't have had any better judgment," Annie said. "And you never called me."

Benson chuckled and said, "We did a little digging around, and I believe we have a line on Ace. We can't look into any of this personally, and I can't confirm it's the right guy, but a source told us Ace hangs out at a poolroom north of the city on occasion. Apparently, a lot of punks hang out there."

Annie's heart was beating fast. "How sure are you it's the right man?"

"I'd count on it. It took a little grease, but our source finally told us that last week, Ace was boasting about a bank job he was considering. And he hangs out in the neighborhood of the bank that was robbed, so it's too coincidental to be anyone else but the right guy."

"Do you have any idea what he looks like?"

"Tall. Muscular. Good-looking."

"That's him," she said, grabbing a notepad and pen. "What's the name of the poolroom?"

"Backstreet Billiards," Benson said. "But be careful, Annie. Our source was practically shaking in his boots and looking over his shoulder when he gave us the information. Apparently, Ace has a violent streak that keeps his cronies in line, and he might be extremely dangerous."

"I'll be careful," Annie said. "I really appreciate this, Detective."

"Don't mention it," Benson said, then paused. "And I mean that. Don't ever mention I called you."

Annie smiled. "I won't."

"Whatever you do with the information is strictly up to you."

"Got it."

The line went dead. Annie hung up the receiver, then picked it up again and dialed Jake's number.

There was no answer, and she waited, letting it ring.

There was still no answer.

Perhaps Jake was busy with something, or maybe his battery was dead. She'd try again later.

For a moment, she considered paying a visit to Backstreet Billiards. She decided against it, at least for the time being. She'd be too conspicuous in a place with the kind of reputation Benson had described, and it might scare away any chance of finding Ace. Besides, she had nothing on the suspect except the word of a cop whose name she couldn't repeat.

She could tell Hank, but then, he'd have no reason to question the suspect at length, and he had nothing substantial they could use to detain him.

She'd have to let Jake handle it. If only she could get hold of him.

She tried his number again. No luck.

Jake would contact her as soon as he was able to, of that she had no doubt, but it didn't lessen her worry or keep her from thinking the unthinkable.

CHAPTER 34

Thursday, 1:48 p.m.

ACE WASN'T HAPPY about having to make another trip downtown. At least, not right now. He had somewhere to be later in the afternoon, and it was important he show up on time.

Though his guys were too weak-minded to take care of it themselves, he was pleased they had his back, contacting him regarding the problem he now faced.

His carefully laid plans were getting messed up by one simple fact—Lincoln was still on the loose and causing him major headaches. He couldn't understand why the police hadn't nailed the guy yet. Surely, now that Lincoln was wanted for two murders, the lazy cops would've brought him in. Or better still, gun him down and save Ace the trouble.

And to make matters worse, he was feeling sore about his pathetic attempt to wipe out Overstone. He'd expected it to be a three-minute job. No more than five. He should've been out of there before Overstone had known what'd hit him. But when all was said and done, he was certain the guy hadn't seen his face. So that was a good thing.

Though there'd been no real harm done in the grand scheme of things, he was kicking himself for being so anxious about the whole Overstone situation. There really hadn't been any hurry to off him. He could always return later and do the job at his leisure, and the results would be the same.

And he never should've trusted Hicks, either. The scumbag had talked. It hadn't taken him long to find that out, and as a consequence of Hicks's big mouth, Lincoln was gunning for him. So, first things first. He had to take care of the PI. Immediately.

Lincoln was a force to be reckoned with, and though his tenacity was admirable, he had to die. Then this whole affair should die with him. Cops don't usually go out of their way to prove a dead man innocent. Especially when they're already convinced he's guilty.

He was pretty sure Lincoln wasn't armed. He knew the guy was a stickler for the rules, and since private citizens, even PIs, can't carry weapons, it made the life of a criminal so much easier.

And it was gonna make killing him a breeze.

It wouldn't be hard to find Lincoln. The guy'd been poking his nose into every bar and late-night establishment in town. One of Ace's underlings would be sure to spot him before long, then it would be lights out.

He pulled his bright red 2007 Mustang into the lane behind Gully's Bar and frowned. His favorite spot was taken by a run-down pickup. He parked further down the lane, then got out and carefully locked up his car. He stopped a second to buff some dust off the hood, not sure why he bothered. The thing was a piece of junk, anyway. Rust all over it.

He strode to the rear of the building and faced the back entrance to the bar. According to his flunkies, Lincoln had been hitting Gully's on a regular basis, and he was liable to show up here at any hour of the day or night. Maybe he was in there now. Better be sure.

Ace pulled out his cell phone and dialed. "I'm outside. He in there?"

"Nope. Been watching for him, though. Ain't showed up yet."

"I'm coming in."

He hung up and stuffed his phone away, then pulled open the door and stepped inside. His crony sat at a table near the back of the room. Ace snapped his fingers at the bartender, then sauntered to the table and dropped into an empty chair. He had a good view of both doors and the rest of the room.

He glanced at the scrawny punk beside him, frowned, and slid his chair away. The guy smelled like yesterday's sweat, his foul odor overpowering even the stale smell of the barroom.

"You need a bath, Harley. You stink."

Harley shrugged. "I don't smell nothin'."

Ace slapped a cigarette from his pack, lit it up, and took a couple of long drags. Smoke curled up and soon caught in a lazy fan overhead, dissipating in the close air. It helped cover Harley's stench. Or maybe he was already getting used to the smell.

The bartender set a foaming glass of beer on the table and nodded at Ace, then went back to the bar. Ace watched him go. He had everybody well trained.

Pool balls cracked together at a table close by, where two dippy-looking punks played for a quarter a ball. Neither one of them knew how to make a decent shot. If he weren't preoccupied at the moment, he'd show them how it was done.

Half-drunk slobs leaned over tables, drinking up their welfare checks. More were glued to stools at the bar. Some sickening eighties tune droned on endlessly in the background.

And Ace sipped at his beer in silence. Waiting.

~*~

JAKE TUGGED ON THE heavy wooden door leading into Gully's Bar. He was looking for that punk Dewey Hicks again. He'd given the guy a day to dig up the whereabouts of Ace, but it seemed like Dewey wasn't about to come through.

Or maybe the guy was afraid to put in an appearance until he had something. Either way, Jake wanted to talk to the useless delinquent again.

He stepped inside and glanced toward the bar. He'd been in here so many times now, the bartender had stopped giving him the curious eye. This time Jake received a quick look, then the proprietor yawned and went back to his job of trading watery beer for cold hard cash.

A pair of guys played pool near the back. Jake squinted through the dim room at a couple more sitting not far from the pool table. One was a skinny runt, and the other was slouched down, a bold red cap pulled forward on his head. Long legs stretched out in front of his body.

Jake had never seen either one of them before.

And Dewey Hicks wasn't around.

The skinny guy got up and wobbled on spindly legs toward Jake. He stopped, cocked his head toward the rear door, and spoke in a squealing voice. "Hicks wants to see you. He's out back. Afraid to show his face in here."

Jake frowned and glanced toward the back of the room. The other guy's arms were crossed on the table, his head resting on top. He'd probably drunk himself to sleep.

He looked back at the scrawny punk and gave a short nod, then followed him out the back door.

Skinny crossed the lane and turned back, ogling Jake, a dry smile splitting his thin face.

Jake looked around. "Where's Hicks?"

Skinny stepped toward him a couple of feet, crossed his arms, and glared into Jake's eyes for a few seconds. Finally, he said, "Hicks ain't here, but Ace wants to meet you real bad."

"And I'm right here." The voice came from directly behind him. It had to be Skinny's companion—the guy with the red cap.

It was Ace.

And Ace was pressing a gun into the back of Jake's head.

In one split second, a million thoughts went through Jake's mind. He'd found Ace, or more accurately, Ace had found him.

But Jake knew the cold steel muzzle leveled at the back of his head wasn't as much of a threat as it seemed to be.

Most guys, like the punk behind him, couldn't hit a barn door if their nose was pressed against it. At least, that's what Jake was hoping, and he was going to give his theory a try. It was better than standing still and waiting for a slug to enter his skull.

He reacted before Ace's small brain could work out what was happening. He dropped to a crouch, then swung around and pushed forward with his powerful leg muscles, slamming his full weight into the gunman.

They both went down. The gun spun through the air, landing with a clunk at Skinny's feet. Jake rolled and sprang forward.

He missed the weapon, but Skinny didn't.

But Skinny didn't know what to do with the thing. While he fumbled to get his finger on the trigger, Jake lunged. He gripped Skinny's bony wrist and wrenched it backwards, freeing the weapon from the guy's feeble grasp with his other hand while the pathetic punk cried out in pain.

Jake stepped back, and Skinny scrambled away.

Jake let him go and spun back toward Ace. But the coward was gone, beating a path down the lane, already nearing the next street.

Jake would never be able to catch him.

He stuffed the pistol behind his belt and watched Ace's back disappear around the corner a couple hundred feet away.

Jake hadn't seen Ace's face, but at least he knew the guy was still hanging around, and he was going to track him down. Sooner or later, their paths would cross. And when they did, Jake wasn't going to be caught by surprise again.

CHAPTER 35

Thursday, 4:14 p.m.

HANK MANEUVERED his Chevy through the beginnings of rush-hour traffic. It was always busy downtown at this time of the day, and the closer they got to the core of the city, the slower everything moved.

Detective King slouched back in the passenger seat and yawned. "At least the guy had the courtesy to kill someone at a decent hour."

Hank rolled his eyes and remained silent. But King had a point. Hopefully, they could do a walk-through and then put the case on hold until CSI had a complete report. Or King could take it on his own. Hank was knee-deep in trying to solve the Overstone case, and he didn't have time to add another murder to his plate at the moment.

But when duty called, he had to respond.

He'd spent the last couple of hours trying to get some information on anyone with a criminal record who went by the name of Ace. He hadn't had much luck. Of the three he'd found, two were incarcerated, and one was dead.

Hank wasn't sure where the name Ace had come from, but it looked like a dead end without a last name.

He squeezed the car between a pair of cruisers parked on either side of a narrow lane, pulling to a stop behind the coroner's van. CSI was there, and investigators were unloading some equipment. Crime scene tape was stretched around. Officers held back curious onlookers.

He and King got out and looked at the abandoned building in front of them.

They were in an older, uncared-for part of town. Graffiti covered the surrounding buildings. Litter lined the fences and grimy walls. The place smelled, the intense odor further fomented by the heat of the glaring afternoon sun.

Hank stepped into the building. The stench inside was even worse. The place had been taken over by vagrants, addicts, and rats. One of the vermin dashed under a pile of garbage. A couple of others were used to human company and paid no attention to the handful of intruders.

The room was lit only by whatever light could work its way through the one grimy window. Someone was in the process of setting up portable lighting, unraveling a long cord that would eventually lead to the closest power source.

CSI was going to have a tough time with this one. Even the best investigator could never separate potential evidence from the piles of trash that filled the room, surrounding the body of the victim who was now lying facedown in the middle of the floor.

Inspectors milled around nonetheless. They would do what they could.

Hank approached Rod Jameson, gave him a curt nod, and got to it. "Any ID?"

Jameson nodded. "Driver's license in the name of Dewey Hicks."

Hank shrugged and looked at King.

"Never heard the name," King said.

The portable lighting came on and the room was filled with dazzling light.

"Shot in the head," Jameson continued, flicking off his flashlight.

"Any witnesses?"

Jameson pointed vaguely toward the exit. "Someone saw the shooter run from the building. An officer's taking his statement, and he's waiting in a cruiser."

"Thanks, Rod," Hank said.

He approached the body and stood beside Nancy Pietek. The ME was in the process of examining the back of the victim's head. Blood and brains were spattered on the floor around the body. The back of his head was a mess.

"Afternoon, Nancy," Hank said.

Nancy turned her head upwards and gave Hank a cheerful smile. "Afternoon, Hank." She stood, turned off her flashlight and slipped off her latex gloves. "It appears the cause of death was a GSW to the back of the head by a small-caliber weapon. Gunshot residue on the victim indicates it was fired from a distance of six to twelve inches."

"Lemme guess," King said with a wry smile. "The manner of death is homicide."

"Sure doesn't look like an accident," Hank said and glanced around. "I don't think there's much else we can do here. Let's go talk to the witness."

Jameson followed them to the door and pointed toward a police car. "There's the guy you want to talk to."

Hank glanced to where Jameson had indicated. The witness had apparently gotten tired of sitting inside the vehicle and had gotten out. He was leaning against the fender, watching the proceedings.

An officer stood nearby. He nodded and stepped aside as Hank and King approached the vehicle.

Hank gave the witness a quick once-over. Probably in his late sixties, the man had probably lived on the streets for a long time. His weather-beaten face, pitted and furrowed by tough times, was proof of a hard life. Oversized clothes hung on his thin frame, a pair of sturdy shoes on his feet.

"I'm Detective Corning," Hank said and motioned toward King. "This is Detective King. Can I get your name?"

The man looked at Hank through deep-set bloodshot eyes. He'd likely imbibed too much whiskey or cheap wine to be reliable, but he was all they had.

He brushed back his matted gray hair with a veined hand and spoke in a faintly slurred voice. "Everybody calls me Slowpoke."

Hank held back a smile. "What's your last name, Slowpoke?"

"Don't remember. Don't know as I ever had one."

"Fair enough," Hank said. "Now, can you tell me what you saw?"

Slowpoke pointed a bony finger toward the building. "I was havin' a wee nap and two guys burst in on me. Snapped me right out of it." He shrugged and pointed to his ear. "Most times, noise don't bother me, but these guys were shouting to wake the dead."

Hank pulled a notepad and pen from his inner pocket and scribbled something down, then looked back at Slowpoke. "What were they shouting about?"

"Couldn't tell. Some kinda argument."

"Then what happened?"

"Then one guy pulled a gun. Couldn't understand what he said, but he was waving it around. I guess he told the other guy to turn around and get on his knees, because he did. Then he shot him and just sauntered out like nothin' happened." Slowpoke shrugged. "Then I skedaddled out of there and got a nice lady to call the police."

"Did the shooter see you?"

"Don't think so. Leastways, he didn't look at me. I was lying down in the corner on a pile of newspaper. Probably didn't see me there, else I'd be shot too. Maybe thought I was a pile of garbage. I was scared to move, I'll tell you that."

"Could you identify the shooter if you saw him again?"

Slowpoke cocked his head to one side. "Can't say as I could. It's kinda dark in there, and these old eyes ain't what they used to be."

"Do your best," Hank said.

Slowpoke looked over Hank's shoulder, his furrowed brow taking on deeper lines of thought. "He was big. I'll say that much. And tall. Had on a red baseball cap."

Hank wrote the information down in his pad.

"Was he muscular?" King asked.

"Yeah, think so. He was big but not fat. Yeah, lots of muscles."

Hank pulled out his cell phone and brought up a photo. He held it up for Slowpoke to see. "Is that him?"

Slowpoke squinted at the phone, then nodded slowly. "Can't be sure, but I think so." He pointed at the photo. "I remember now. Like I said, he had a cap on, but pretty sure his hair was short like that, too. It was pretty dark."

Hank glanced at the photo of Jake on his cell phone, then looked at his partner. King crossed his arms and frowned at the phone.

Hank turned back to Slowpoke. "Is there anything else you can tell us?"

The old man shook his head. "That's all I saw."

Hank turned to the officer, who'd been lounging nearby listening to the conversation. "Did you get his statement?"

The officer nodded, opened the door of the cruiser, and returned with a clipboard. He handed Hank a sheet of paper. "I wrote down what he said, and he signed it."

Hank looked at the scrawl at the bottom of the page, then rolled it up and tucked it into his pocket. He spoke to Slowpoke. "You've been a big help. Thanks for your time."

Slowpoke smiled for the first time. "Just doin' my part. Hope you catch him. God knows it ain't safe enough for folks like me on the streets anymore."

The detectives went back to Hank's car and got in. Hank started the car thoughtfully. Things weren't looking good for Jake.

"What do you think?" King asked. "I know Slowpoke couldn't give a positive ID, but he was pretty sure it was Jake."

Hank's lips formed a grim line. "We know Jake's down here somewhere, according to two separate police reports. But I can't see it. Jake's not a killer."

"I'm starting to wonder," King said.

Hank pulled from the lane and turned onto the side street. He didn't want to admit it, but he was having second thoughts as well, and he wanted to find out more about Dewey Hicks. He needed to find out if Hicks's murder was related to the Overstone case, where he fit in, and why he'd ended up dead.

Unless CSI got lucky and turned up something useful, all he had to go on was a contaminated crime scene and the word of a drunk.

CHAPTER 36

Thursday, 6:12 p.m.

LISA KRUNK HAD been following Niles Overstone around for most of the day. As far as she knew, he was the only person who might have any knowledge of what the murders were all about.

After she'd gotten wind of the attempt on Overstone's life through her source in the police department, she and Don had raced to the scene. But she hadn't been able to obtain any information that was going to do her any good. The police had been as tight-lipped as usual, and the few shots Don had gotten were practically useless.

The cops had sealed off the home again, and she'd been unable to get a lead on Overstone's current whereabouts. She only knew that, though several shots had been fired, no one had been injured, and the gunman had escaped.

But with Overstone having no access to his house, Lisa had been sure he'd eventually return to the very spot where he'd spent his nights after his wife's shooting.

If someone was going to shoot at him again, she wanted to be there.

Leaving Don with the van, she'd taken her seldom-used silver Corolla and headed to Richmond Inn. She'd recognized the white Lexus parked in front of cabin seven, the same unit Overstone had occupied before.

After taking a subtle peek through the window and confirming Overstone was inside, she had returned to her car and waited.

In the hours following, she'd tailed him to a restaurant for lunch, then to Richmond Funeral Home. He'd met an overweight middle-aged woman outside, and after the woman had butted out a smoke, the two had gone inside the building. They'd spent a couple of hours inside, then Overstone had returned to his room.

While Lisa had watched outside his unit, she'd placed a phone call. She'd found out a wake for Merrilla Overstone would take place that evening, with the funeral to be held early the next afternoon.

That was when she'd made plans to attend both events. Discreetly, of course.

While waiting, she'd kept one ear tuned to the police radio tucked under her dash. There'd been a shooting in an abandoned building downtown, and after giving the information some serious thought, she had decided not to go. Not only was news of a shooting in that neighborhood not in the least unusual, but gang wars and punks killing other punks weren't the kind of stories most people cared about. Besides, by the time Don got there, and they waded their way through rush-hour traffic, everything would be wrapped up and sealed off.

She had decided she might as well wait it out and waste her time here rather than there.

Then, after a boring time of it, at five-thirty, she'd followed Overstone back to the funeral home. He'd met the same chubby woman, and the two of them had gone directly inside. Other than them, she hadn't seen anyone else enter or leave the building.

Maybe the Overstones didn't have a lot of friends.

And now, as she sat in her car across the street from the funeral home, she kept an eagle eye on the building. A couple of cops were lounging around outside the entranceway. Perhaps the police had assumed, as she did, that Overstone might be the target of a killer at his own wife's wake.

She had half a mind to take her camera, slip inside, and take a few shots. But for some reason her viewers didn't take kindly to that sort of thing. Though it would be nice to be on the scene if something went down, she decided not to. The cops would likely bar her from entering, anyway.

A car pulled into the lot, and she grabbed her binoculars, zooming in on the face of a man as he stepped from the vehicle. It was some old guy, and he didn't look like he meant any harm. It was probably someone Overstone worked with. The cops waved him into the building, and he disappeared from view.

A handful of people came and went, and Lisa snapped their pictures out of boredom. She was starting to think she'd wasted her time.

She listened to the police radio. Nothing of interest appeared to be happening elsewhere in the city. It was a slow news day, and she might as well hang around.

When a bright red Mustang pulled into the lot, Lisa barely paid it any attention. Then her eyes widened when a man got out, adjusted his tie, and strode toward the building.

It was Jake.

What was he doing here? Had something happened she wasn't aware of? Had Jake been cleared?

She swung her binoculars into action. He was walking too fast for her to focus on him, and by the time she could, she only caught a quick glimpse of his side view as he climbed the steps and entered the building.

Though it wasn't something she often concerned herself with, she couldn't help but notice how handsome he looked. All dressed up in a sharp black suit, close-cropped hair, tall and clean-shaven with chiseled features. She'd never seen him look so good before.

She chided herself for thinking about unimportant matters and turned back to the subject at hand.

Why was he here?

Had she been wrong about Jake? Was he planning to kill Overstone? And why wasn't Annie with him?

But then, the cops had barely given Jake a look when he went inside, and she was confused about what it all meant.

She watched and waited, holding her camera steady. She planned to zoom in and get some shots of Jake as he left. If he was up to no good, chances were he'd be leaving in an almighty hurry. She had to be ready.

She leaned forward, focused, zoomed in, and waited.

Then the door opened, and he stepped into view and hurried down the steps. The camera clicked a dozen times before his back was to her. She took a few more shots as he climbed into the Mustang and sped away.

Lisa zoomed in on the cops outside the door. They were chatting and laughing. One was having a smoke. If something had happened inside, they would've known about it by now.

She turned her attention to the camera, worked her way through the images, and stopped at the picture she'd taken as Jake exited the building.

Her eyes widened and her mouth dropped open when she zoomed in on his face.

CHAPTER 37

Thursday, 8:18 p.m.

IT APPEARED JAKE wasn't going to be home for breakfast in the morning. Annie had missed their family meals the last couple of days. Her thoughts had been consumed with her husband, and though he was foremost in her mind, she couldn't neglect Matty.

While preparing their supper, she'd found she was running low on a lot of items. She'd been so busy trying to help solve Jake's dilemma that she'd let things slip.

She decided to take a run to Mortino's and stock up on some necessities. The store would be closing soon, and she wanted to get her shopping out of the way so she could concentrate on the task at hand bright and early the next morning.

She hustled Matty outside, then locked up the house and hurried to the Corolla. It was starting to get dark, the lowering sun displaying reds and oranges as it dropped behind the roof of the house.

Matty jumped into the passenger seat and fastened his seat belt, then turned to his mother, a worried look on his face. "Mom, Dad's in some kind of trouble, isn't he?"

It wasn't a question as much as a statement, and she knew he suspected there was more to Jake's absence than the little she had explained to him.

Annie started the car and sat back, choosing her words with care before turning to face her son.

"Matty, there are certain people who think your father killed a man. We know he didn't, but whoever did made it look like it was your father. He can't come home right now. But soon."

"Can't Uncle Hank do something?"

Annie put her hand on her son's shoulder. "He's trying, Matty. We're all trying. But Uncle Hank's a police officer, and he has to do what the law tells him to."

Matty frowned. "Is there anything I can do?"

Annie smiled. "As a matter of fact, all I need you to do is be strong until this is all over. That'll help both of us." Matty's frown lessened and she spoke again. "We're getting close to finding the real killer, and this'll be over soon, and your father will be back."

Matty nodded slowly. "I guess I can wait another day."

Annie pulled from the driveway and onto the street. Her son had faith in his father. It wasn't that she didn't, but the situation was a lot more complicated than she'd expected.

She was worried she still hadn't been able to reach Jake on

the phone, and her concern that something might've happened to him was growing by the minute.

She glanced in her rearview mirror as she turned off Carver Street onto Main. A red Mustang seemed to be following rather closely.

She switched lanes, and it followed. If it was the police, the driver was being a lot more obvious about it this time, and she had an uneasy feeling it wasn't a cop.

Annie touched the gas and the Toyota sped up. The Mustang lost ground, then she heard the rumble of its engine, and the vehicle was back on her tail. And this time it was closer.

Now she had no doubt the vehicle was following her. And if he was trying to frighten her, he was doing a good job of it. But Annie feared the driver might have more in mind than giving her a good scare.

She glanced at Matty. The boy was looking out the side window, oblivious to the potential threat, and she felt indignant someone would endanger a child's life.

Traffic was clear to her left, so she wrenched the wheel hard and swerved into the lane. He followed, now right behind her again.

Three seconds later, she turned the wheel to the right, bounced across two lanes, and took an exit to the four-lane highway leading out of town.

Matty's head spun toward her, alarm in his voice. "Why're you driving like a maniac, Mom?"

He must've noticed her eyes glued to the rearview mirror. He turned toward the backseat, then shouted, "Watch out, Mom."

She'd seen it, too. The Mustang had hit the brakes and spun fully around, and now it was gaining on her from behind. She had an open road ahead of her, but her Corolla could never outrun a Mustang. There was no point in even trying, but she couldn't just come to a stop.

"Hang on, Matty!"

She pushed the gas pedal to the floor. The speedometer edged up as the Toyota sped ahead.

Thirty. Forty. Now fifty.

The car jolted. Her head whacked into the headrest. He'd rammed her from behind. Tires squealed and the vehicle went into a fishtail.

She hung on. Jake might drive fast and appear to be a crazy driver to the untrained, but he knew how to handle a vehicle in just about any situation. And he'd taught her some of the finer points of driving. She put that knowledge to use now and brought the vehicle under control.

"He's way behind now, Mom."

He had lost ground when he'd slammed into them, but he'd soon gain it again.

She kept her speed under forty, making another hit from behind easier to control. He couldn't keep this up forever.

Annie strained to get a glimpse of the Mustang's license plate. The car was too far behind now, too close before.

The attacking vehicle crept closer, then swung into the passing lane and slowed. Annie spun her head to the left as the vehicle pulled alongside.

The passenger-side window of the Mustang was open, and the driver had a pistol pointed directly at her.

The gun exploded. She slammed on the brakes, and the Mustang shot ahead. She whipped the steering wheel to the left, and tires squealed. The rear end spun around, and the vehicle faced back toward the way she'd come.

Annie poured on the gas and glanced in the rearview mirror. The driver of the Mustang had tried a similar high-speed U-turn and failed. The nose of his vehicle was tipped into the shallow ditch at the edge of the road.

He wasn't down and out, and she had but a few precious seconds before he could spin back onto the highway and overtake her again.

"He's coming, Mom."

It was less than a quarter mile back to Main Street, and Annie pushed her new car to the limit. As she approached Main, she slowed to allow a lazy car to drift through the intersection, then spun in behind it. She touched the gas and surged ahead, passed the vehicle, then narrowly missed another one as she took a quick left onto a side street.

She'd made it.

The Toyota cruised down the street, and Annie kept an eye in her rearview mirror. She'd lost the Mustang.

"You did it, Mom. Nice driving."

Annie circled the block, ending back on Main. The Mustang was nowhere in sight. She pulled into a strip plaza and sat back, closing her eyes.

"Mom, you should call Uncle Hank."

Annie looked at Matty and nodded. "Give me a second to catch my breath."

She took a few deep breaths to calm her jangling nerves

and thumping heart, then pulled out her cell phone and dialed Hank's number. When he answered, she filled him in as quickly as possible on what'd taken place. "I'm not sure what year the Mustang was," she said. "Fairly recent, and I never had a chance to see the license plate."

"I'll put out a BOLO immediately," Hank said. "It's bound to have some front end damage. A scratch or two at least. How's your vehicle?"

"I haven't taken a look yet, but there must be some damage."

"You're safe, and that's the main thing," Hank said. "Did you see the driver's face?"

Annie hesitated. "He looked a little like Jake. You know—clean cut. Much the same features. And he was wearing a suit and tie."

"You'd better go home. I'll send a car around to watch the house overnight. You'll be safe, and they'll stay there as long as is necessary."

"Hank, I'm betting this is all connected to the Overstone affair. I have no doubt."

"Then let me get on it. As soon as we bring him in, we'll find out what it's all about."

Annie hung up the phone and looked at Matty. Her son had unfastened his seat belt, and he was turned around in the seat, keeping an eye through the back window.

"I guess he's gone, Mom. But Uncle Hank'll get him."

She hoped Matty was right, and though she hadn't mentioned it to Hank, there was no doubt in her mind the driver of the Mustang was the guy Jake was looking for.

It had to be Ace.

And if it was, the maniac had already proved himself to be a murderer, and Annie feared the killer wouldn't let up until he finished the job.

CHAPTER 38

Thursday, 8:39 p.m.

ANNIE KEPT A CLOSE watch around her as she pulled down Carver Street and into the driveway of her home. The Mustang hadn't returned.

She hurried Matty into the house. If the man she was sure was Ace was lurking nearby, she feared he wouldn't be deterred by the presence of a child. His actions had already proven that.

Going into the kitchen, she sat at the table and called Jake's number. She was caught off guard when he answered.

"I was worried when I couldn't get hold of you," she said. "I was imagining the worst had happened."

"I was about to call you. I didn't realize the battery was dead at first," he explained. "And when I did, I had to find a safe place to charge it up. I ended up at a little coffee shop where they have a recharging service for customers."

"I got a call from Detective Benson," Annie said.

"I had a talk with him and O'Day, as well. I hope he had something for you."

"He told me Ace hangs around a place called Backstreet Billiards. It's not far from the bank that was robbed."

"That's uptown," Jake said. "I'm not even close to there."

"Can you take a cab? The public still isn't aware the police are looking for you."

"Should be able to. But I have no way of knowing where Ace might be. He was down here this afternoon. I met him briefly, but I wasn't able to grab him."

For a moment, she considered not telling him about her run-in with Ace. He had enough to worry about. But if Ace was up here, and Jake was downtown, he might be wasting his time.

"Jake, does Ace look somewhat like you?"

"He's about as tall as me," Jake said. "Not quite as muscular, but close. I didn't see his face, but I doubt he had my charming good looks."

Annie hesitated. "I think we met him."

"We?"

Annie explained, purposely minimizing the extent of the danger they'd been in. "We're fine," she said. "But Hank's sending a car to watch the house."

"What kind of vehicle was he driving?"

"A red Mustang."

"A red Mustang?" Jake said. "There was a red Mustang

parked in the lane where I had a run-in with Ace. He must've returned for it later. I should've known, but the thing looked like it'd been abandoned."

"You had no way of knowing it was his," Annie said. "But now you do."

"Any idea what year it was?"

"No. But it wasn't very old. Maybe ten years."

"Close enough. I'm gonna find out where Backstreet Billiards is and get up there this evening."

"Keep an eye on your battery," Annie said.

"I will."

"And be careful."

"Always," Jake said. "Let me speak to Matty."

Annie called Matty into the room and handed him the phone. The boy's face lit up when she told him who was on the other end.

She watched her son as he laughed and joked around with his father. Jake was doing a good job of putting his boy at ease.

"Dad said he'll be home soon," Matty said, hanging up and handing her the phone. He ran into the living room, a cheerful look on his face.

When the doorbell rang a few minutes later, Annie went to the door and peered through the viewer. She frowned. It was Lisa Krunk. The newswoman was the last person she wanted to see at the moment.

Annie sighed and opened the door. Lisa had an urgent look on her face and a manila envelope in one hand.

"I need to speak to you. Can I come in?"

Annie opened the door, and Lisa stepped into the foyer, handing Annie the envelope. "I think you'll be very interested in this."

Taking the envelope, Annie opened it and slipped out a pair of five-by-seven photos, both the same. She caught her breath. "Where'd you get these?"

"At the funeral home. He came to Merrilla Overstone's wake."

Annie looked closer at the picture. It was the same man who'd tried to run them off the road, and he was wearing the same suit. It was Ace, but what'd he been doing at the wake?

"I thought it was Jake at first," Lisa said. "Until I got a close-up view. That's when I put two and two together. This might be the man you're looking for. From a distance, anyone might think it was Jake."

"I think that's exactly what happened, Lisa. Witnesses who were familiar with Jake IDed him because the real killer looks like him."

Lisa shrugged. "It almost had me fooled." Her face took on a smug look. "But of course, I knew better."

"Was he driving a red Mustang?" Annie asked.

"Yes. How'd you know?"

"Never mind. But there's no doubt now, Lisa. He's connected to the Overstone shootings somehow, and this is the guy we're looking for."

"Then I'm happy I did my part," Lisa said. She waved a hand, then turned and stepped outside. "I hope it helps."

Annie shut the door. There was no doubt she could ID Ace as the driver of the red Mustang, but as far as she knew, there was still no solid proof linking him to the bank robbery, the shooting of Merrilla Overstone, or the attempt on Niles Overstone's life. The video evidence was unclear, and the witnesses were unsure.

She looked at her watch. It was getting late, and Matty had school tomorrow, but she had to get one of these photos to Jake as soon as possible.

CHAPTER 39

Thursday, 9:07 p.m.

JAKE MADE HIS WAY to the coffee shop where he'd gotten his burner phone charged earlier. After Annie had called him back to tell him about the photo, he'd given her the address of the shop, and they'd made plans to meet there.

He was looking forward to seeing his wife and son again.

And of course, he was anxious to see the photo of Ace. The sooner he got out of the pickle he was in, the better.

While he waited, he took the opportunity to top up his cell phone. Then he pulled out the iPad. Considering everything he'd been through the last couple of days, he was surprised he'd managed to hold on to it. It still worked, so he looked up the exact location of Backstreet Billiards.

He was familiar with the name; it wasn't far from home and the area where he'd spent most of his life. But it hadn't been in business long and, like the name suggested, it was located on one of the backstreets half a mile from the Commerce Bank.

Jake gulped the remainder of his coffee and grabbed his phone and charger. A white Corolla had pulled into a parking spot and blinked its brake lights three times.

It was Annie.

As he approached the vehicle, Matty hopped between the seats and dove into the back. Jake paused and crouched down by the rear of the vehicle, giving it an inspection. The bumper had received a solid whack, but once it was replaced, the vehicle would be as good as new.

He got in the car and grinned at his family. Matty wrapped his arms around Jake's neck from behind. "Hey, Dad," was all the boy said.

Jake freed himself from his son's grasp and turned around, mussing up Matty's hair. Then the boy let out an impatient sigh and waited while Jake greeted his wife with an extended kiss.

Annie pointed to the glove compartment. "The picture's in there."

Jake removed the envelope and pulled out the photo. He frowned at the image, then at Annie. "He doesn't look like me at all."

Annie chuckled. "Some people think he does."

Matty sat in the middle of the seat and leaned forward. "When're you coming home, Dad?"

Jake held up the photo. "As soon as I find this guy."

"Is he the one who killed the other man?"

"Yes. And I need to put a stop to him."

Annie started the car. "Instead of you taking a cab, I can give you a ride there," she said. "I'd let you take the car after we get home, but there're two officers in an unmarked vehicle watching the house. I don't know how we'd be able to do the switch."

"That's okay. Just get me there. I'll take care of the rest." Jake glanced around the parking area. "Are you sure they didn't follow you?"

Annie shook her head and backed out, pulling onto the street. "No. I told them I'd be right back, and they didn't move." She paused, then said, "I'd go with you, but I have no one to watch Matty."

"It's okay. Ace is too dangerous, anyway," Jake said. "But I know how to handle him."

Jake directed Annie by the quickest route. Traffic was light, and a few minutes later, he pointed to the side of the street. "Pull over here. I'll walk the rest of the way."

Annie pulled over and stopped. "I'll be waiting by the phone," she said as he jumped out.

"Don't wait up. I might be a while."

"Just call me."

"I'll call," Jake said, then stepped back and watched his family drive away.

He took a look around, then turned and went down the sidewalk, heading for Crestwood Avenue and Backstreet Billiards.

If he was lucky enough to come across Ace, he realized they could always call the police and have the guy arrested. But Jake wanted much more than that. He wanted to nail the guy for two murders.

But to do that, he'd have to get a confession. That might

mean putting himself in extreme danger. It wasn't something he was so hot on doing, but if that's what it took to keep his family safe, he had no other choice.

Jake stopped at Crestwood and peered down the street. There were several cars parked along the edge of the road, but there was no red Mustang. This might not be as easy as he'd hoped.

A couple of punks stood at the front of a vehicle. Faint sounds of their conversation carried to Jake.

He eased down the dimly lit street. Thirty feet from the building, he paused in the shadow of a large tree and waited.

A souped-up Chevelle roared around the corner and zoomed down the street, well over the speed limit. The driver hit the brakes hard and pulled the vehicle to the shoulder. Two guys got out and crossed the street to the pool hall.

He considered going inside, but if the place was filled with punks like Benson had said, his presence would stand out. Besides, it didn't appear Ace was in there.

Jake fingered the gun tucked behind his belt. Ace's old gun. And it was fully loaded. The last thing he wanted to do was to use it—except for defense, or to get someone to talk, but he'd be loath to fire it unless absolutely necessary.

But if Ace had replaced his lost weapon with another, things could get hairy, and Jake might have to reconsider.

People came and went, and fifteen minutes later, Jake was wondering if Ace was planning to put in an appearance.

The guy could be anywhere.

Then a red Mustang breezed down the street and pulled over. Three guys got out. Two of them were short in comparison to the third.

From where Jake waited, he couldn't make out any facial features, but the tall guy—the driver—had to be Ace.

Jake had hoped to catch him alone. With three guys to contend with, the odds weren't in Jake's favor, especially if they were armed.

Easing forward a few feet, Jake ducked behind a concrete garbage receptacle and peered around. The three guys crossed the street, Ace out in front. And it was Ace. They paused under a streetlight and Ace lit a smoke. Jake squinted at the skinny guy. It was the same wimp Jake had encountered the last time he'd run into Ace. He didn't recognize the third guy.

Jake pulled out his cell phone and snapped a couple of pictures.

The punks went into the pool hall, the door closed behind them, and Jake had to come up with a new plan.

When the door opened again fifteen minutes later and Ace stepped out, Jake was ready. He moved from the shadows at the side of the doorway, the pistol in his hand. One arm went around Ace's throat, the other hand holding the weapon to the killer's ribs.

"Don't move, Ace."

Ace struggled to get a view of his assailant.

"I'm Jake Lincoln, and we're going for a little drive."

"I ain't going anywhere with you."

Jake hung on, digging the pistol into Ace's ribs. "I'm pretty sure you are."

Ace battled to work Jake's arm from around his throat. The guy was strong, there was no doubt about that, and Jake was having a hard time keeping his grip. He could only use one hand; the other was holding the pistol. But Ace had two free hands and was fighting for his life.

Jake stuffed the weapon behind his belt. It wasn't doing him any good. The punk knew Jake would never shoot him.

Ace struggled to bring one hand behind his back. He was going for a weapon. Jake got there first and removed the pistol. He flung it away, then twisted the arm, causing Ace to howl in pain.

A voice came from behind. "Back off, Lincoln."

Jake held on and spun around to face the owner of the voice, dragging Ace with him. It was the third guy, and he had a pistol pointed at Jake. Skinny stood beside him, and he had a gun as well.

The guy moved in and stopped five feet away. "Let him go."

"Shoot him," Ace said. "He ain't gonna do nothin'."

The punk moved closer. Skinny stayed back.

Jake had no choice but to let Ace go free. Anything else would only end in a standoff. With three guys about to surround him, and all of them armed with pistols and willing to kill, Jake would be sure to come out the loser.

"Gimme your gun," the guy said.

Jake removed the weapon from his belt and tossed it onto the pavement, then held up his free hand in surrender. "I'll let him go," he said. "Just don't move."

Keeping his other arm around Ace's throat, Jake dragged him back a few feet from the gunman. Then he let go and gave him a violent shove forward. Ace fell into the shooter, and Jake leaped out of the line of fire and raced up the sidewalk to the corner.

No one followed him, but Jake was disappointed in the outcome of his plan.

He really wished he could call Hank. Ace would be more careful in the future, and Jake might not get a second chance.

In a minute, the Mustang roared by and disappeared from view.

He dropped down onto the sidewalk and leaned back against the brick wall, thoroughly disgusted. Pulling out his cell phone, he dialed Annie's number. She'd be disappointed as well, but she'd know, as he did, he was far from giving up.

Tomorrow would be another day.

CHAPTER 40

DAY 5 - Friday, 7:33 a.m.

HANK SAT AT THE kitchen table in his apartment, deep in thought. He'd worked into the wee hours of the morning and been up with the sun. The case had been weighing heavily on his mind, and he knew he had a decision to make.

He'd discussed it at length with Amelia last evening, and her opinion had cemented his resolution. As soon as he got to the precinct, he was going to ask Diego if he could withdraw from the case. He could no longer do his job.

Sure, he could do half a job. He could follow the evidence and see where it led, but the evidence led straight to Jake. And that's where the problem started and his resolve stopped.

It was true there was some circumstantial evidence in Jake's favor, but in the eyes of the law, it wasn't enough to outweigh the rest. It wasn't sufficient to warrant giving Jake his freedom. That wasn't Hank's decision to make.

Amelia had been fully on Jake's side, convinced he was a victim of a malicious frame. She could never bring herself to admit someone who'd endangered his own life to save the life of her daughter could be so cold-hearted.

And Hank agreed.

Though Hank was a well-trained cop, with more experience on the job than most, Amelia was so much more intuitive than he was. She saw things he couldn't, and this was only one of the countless reasons he loved her.

For the third time that week, he opened his briefcase and slipped out a small velvet-covered box. Flipping up the top, he looked at the sparkling diamond ring inside.

What was he waiting for? Was it because she outclassed him? Not really. Sure, she had a lot of money, but she was as down-to-earth as he was.

It wasn't the small size of the diamond that bothered him, and he knew it wouldn't faze her for a second.

And it wasn't because he didn't know what her answer would be. He'd never been surer of anything in his life.

But something was holding him back, and he vowed to solve the mystery as soon as his current dilemma was taken care of.

Hank tucked the ring safely back into a pocket of the briefcase and snapped the case closed. He looked at his watch. He'd better get to work.

Diego wasn't in his office when Hank arrived at the precinct. Yappy explained that the captain had been delayed due to a family matter and was running a few minutes late. Hank nodded and went to his desk.

He set his briefcase beside his chair, then retrieved Jake's camera from the evidence box and took it to Callaway's desk. He set the camera in front of the whiz and sat in the guest chair.

Callaway looked at the camera. "What's up with that?"

"It's Jake's," Hank said. "All the images have been erased. Is there a possibility you can look at the memory card and recover any deleted pictures?"

Callaway picked up the camera. "As long as they haven't been overwritten, there's always a chance."

"I need to see what was on there ASAP. It's important."

"It might take a while. Leave it with me." Callaway flipped open a small cover on the camera, removed a memory card from the slot, and turned it over in his fingers. "It's a thirty-two-gig SD memory card. It shouldn't be a problem. I'll get right on it, Hank."

"Thanks, Callaway."

Hank went to the break room. Detective King sat at the table in his usual position, one running shoe cocked up on the tabletop, a cup of coffee in his hand.

"Morning, King," Hank said and King grunted.

Hank went straight to the coffeepot. Someone had made a fresh pot and, for a change, it didn't look half bad. He poured himself a cup and sat at the table opposite his partner. He took a sip of his drink. It didn't taste half bad either.

"No word on the street about Dewey Hicks," King said. "Guys I talked to don't know who he was."

"Keep on it. There's a connection somewhere." Hank told King about what he hoped to find on the memory card. "I've come to believe Jake's totally innocent. I've been over this a thousand times, and there's too much that doesn't make sense."

"Such as?"

"The burner phone found under the car seat, for example. First of all, why was it necessary, and secondly, why would he put it there? And it didn't have Jake's prints on it."

"True," King said. "But if he was up to no good, he might've been wearing gloves."

"Then where are they? They weren't in the car or in the house. We have everything he was wearing and everything he was carrying. And why was there no blood spatter on his clothes? Mrs. Overstone was shot from a short distance away. All that was found was GSR. That's consistent with Jake's story."

"What about Merrilla Overstone's verbal statement?"

"She had to have been delusional. If the real killer looked like Jake, she might've been confused. When you have a bullet in your chest, it's hard to think straight. And the guy who IDed Hicks's killer couldn't make a positive identification. And neither could anyone at the bank robbery."

"I'm totally with you, Hank," King said. "I just don't know how we can prove it."

Hank sat forward. "By helping Jake find the real killer."

"Jake's a wanted man. We've been skirting around it now, but if we have contact with him, and we don't make an attempt to arrest him, that's not exactly protocol. As you know, both of us could lose our jobs for that."

"Look, King, we don't need to have any contact with him. But Annie's convinced it's a guy named Ace, and so is Jake. Don't forget, he tried to run Annie off the road. We have enough to bring him in for questioning, but I need to find out who he is first." Hank paused and took a sip of his coffee. "I'm going to tell Diego I need to withdraw from the case for personal reasons, then take a few days off and figure this out."

"And you want me to take over the investigation?"

"That's the idea."

King shrugged. "If you think that's the best way to go, I'm game."

Hank stood. "I'll talk to Diego. He should be here by now."

Diego was in his office when Hank returned to the precinct floor. "Can I see you a minute?" Hank asked, tapping on the open office door.

The captain hung his jacket on a hook and turned around, waving Hank in. He straightened his tie, sat behind his desk, and leaned forward. "What is it, Hank?"

Hank sat down and paused a moment before speaking. He hoped he was doing the right thing. "Captain, I need to withdraw from the Overstone case. It's too personal for me."

Diego frowned. "I don't have anyone else who can handle it."

"I talked to Detective King. He's willing to take over."

"Hank, you know King as well as I do. He has some good points, but he lacks drive. And he lacks finesse." Diego leaned back and removed his cap, setting it on the desk. He smoothed back his dark hair. "This case is personal for us all, Hank."

"Then I'm asking you to withdraw the manhunt for Jake and we can all sort this out together."

"I can't do that. In fact, I'm a little disturbed Jake hasn't been brought in by now." Diego cleared his throat. "I'm planning a press conference at noon to announce it to the public, and I'm going to personally see efforts to find him are doubled."

"Can't you give it another twenty-four hours, Captain?"

Diego shook his head adamantly. "Can't do it. This has gone on long enough. And if that Hicks character is connected to this case, then we have enough bodies on our hands already." He leaned forward and pointed a finger. "I can't let you withdraw from this case. That's not an option. Nobody withdraws from any case unless I tell them to."

Hank tried once more. "I need to take some vacation time, Captain."

"After this is over, you can take all the time you want." Diego paused and spoke in a flat voice. "Sorry, Hank. I need you on this."

"Yes, Captain," Hank said. He stood and blew out a long breath. "I'll get back at it."

Hank left Diego's office and glanced at Callaway. The young cop was leaning into his monitor, tapping furiously on the keyboard. If there was anything to be found on the memory card, Callaway was the one who could find it.

He went into the break room, where King sat in the same spot, now holding a half-eaten blueberry muffin in one hand.

"Diego won't allow me to withdraw," Hank said, dropping into a chair.

"Not surprised. And you can bet he's gonna be keeping an eagle eye on you from now on. On both of us."

"Then we'll have to do this by the book," Hank said. "And if we don't come up with something soon, Jake's gonna be in big trouble."

CHAPTER 41

Friday, 9:13 a.m.

JAKE OPENED THE door to Backstreet Billiards and stepped inside. The place had just opened and it was dead. Paying customers would come later in the day, and the punks would show up again when the sun went down.

An elderly man was tying a big green garbage bag he'd pulled from a can near the front counter. Litter on the floor awaited a nearby vacuum cleaner, soon to be put to good use. A whistling fan in the center of the room cleared away the stale smell of yesterday's cigarette smoke. Music played softly in the background.

The man set the bag aside and looked up as Jake approached. "Morning," he said, flashing a grin and revealed a gaping hole where a tooth should have been.

"Morning," Jake said. "I'm looking for a friend. I'm hoping you can help me."

The man straightened and scratched his balding head,

271

studying Jake's face. "You don't look like a guy with friends who'd hang around here."

Jake grinned and pulled the photo of Ace from his back pocket. He held it up. "He's not exactly a friend, but I need to find him."

The man squinted at Jake. "You a cop?"

"Private detective."

"Can't say as I've ever seen him," the man said, looking back at the photo. "Don't look familiar."

Jake pulled out his cell phone and tapped his way to Skinny's picture. He zoomed in on the face and held it up. "What about this guy?"

The aging man pursed his lips a moment, then nodded. "Seen him around sometimes during the day. Probably comes in mostly in the evening. I don't work the evening shift. Too rough and noisy around here." He glanced around the room and shrugged. "I like it quiet."

"Do you know his name?"

"I might." He paused and frowned at Jake. "Might know where he lives, too. Trouble is, they don't pay me enough here to remember stuff like that."

Jake shoved a hand into his pocket and removed what money he had left. He peeled off a twenty and held it out. "This help you remember?"

The man took the bill and held it up to the light, then stuffed it into his shirt pocket. "Seems to be coming to me now," he said. "He hangs around with another guy a lot. Heard them talking one day. He lives in an apartment building, and the only one round here is next street over. Name's Harley."

"First or last?"

"Last."

"You're sure?"

"Yup."

"Any idea where he works?"

The man chuckled. "Guys like him don't work. Maybe at nighttime, if you know what I mean."

Jake knew what he meant. "Thanks," he said, turning to leave. "You've been a big help."

"Hey, mister," the man called. "You ain't gonna go blabbin' about who told you, are you?"

"Not a word," Jake said.

He stepped outside, not sure exactly how to proceed. But he knew where Harley lived, and that was a start. He looked at his watch. The guy was a night owl and would probably still be sleeping.

That was good.

Jake hurried around the block to the next street and gazed at the two-story building where he hoped Harley lived. The building was about as run-down as a building can be, blending in perfectly with the rest of the neighborhood.

The building had no security lock, and when he stepped inside, he was disappointed to see there was no directory of tenants in the lobby. Harley could be in any one of the ten or so units. He hoped somebody knew which one the punk lived in.

A sign on the door of apartment 101 notified him that was where the superintendent lived. It was the best place to start.

He banged on the door and it opened a minute later. A

middle-aged man tightened the belt of his housecoat and looked at him through bleary eyes.

"I'm looking for Harley," Jake said.

The man pointed a thumb toward the ceiling. "Upstairs. Top of the steps." Then the door closed.

Jake took the steps two at a time and stopped in front of the first door. He twisted the knob. The door was locked. He knocked.

No answer.

He waited a moment and knocked again.

"Who is it?" a sleepy voice called.

"It's Ace," Jake said, hoping his imitation was good enough to do the trick.

It was. The doorknob rattled and the door moved inward, and the skinny punk spoke. "What're you doing up so early?"

Jake pushed the door open all the way and stepped inside. Harley moved back and blinked a couple of times, then his eyes widened when he realized who it was.

"You're gonna tell me where I can find Ace," Jake said. He took a handful of Harley's t-shirt and rammed him against the wall. "And you have about three seconds to tell me."

Harley cowered back. His eyes darted around, then he looked up at Jake towering over him. His voice quivered. "Ace'll kill me."

"Not if I kill you first."

The skinny punk glanced toward the door, then back at Jake.

Jake released his hold and wrapped his fingers around Harley's throat. "You're running out of time," he said, tightening his grip to make his point.

Harley remained silent, glaring and blinking.

Jake squeezed a little harder, hoisted the punk up almost off his feet, and held him firmly against the wall.

Harley gasped for air and held up a hand in surrender. "Okay. Okay."

Jake let go and straightened his back, crossing his arms.

Harley bit his lip. "Two twenty Crestwood."

"Does he live alone?"

"He ... he lives with his mother."

Jake frowned. "What's Ace's real name?"

"Just Ace. That all everybody calls him."

"Last name?"

"Irish. Ace Irish. That's all I know."

Jake narrowed his eyes and leaned in. "If you tell him I was here, then I'll have to come back."

Harley nodded frantically.

Jake leaned down closer and glared into Harley's eyes. "I mean that."

Harley kept nodding.

Jake glared at the skinny punk a little longer, then turned and left the apartment. Harley's door slammed as Jake hurried down the stairs.

He made his way back to Crestwood Avenue. The house at 220 was on the same side of the street as the pool hall, and a couple of blocks further down. He stopped across the street from the house and studied it.

A tumbledown garage stood near the rickety bungalow, its roof sagging and ready to cave in. A narrow gravel lane ran between it and the house. At the front of the dwelling, a pair of windows faced the street. He watched the windows a moment and saw no movement.

Jake crossed the road, pushed open the unlocked access door to the garage and peered inside. The building was empty. Continuing on, he went up the lane beside the house, then stopped short at the corner of the building. A red Mustang sat at the back of the house. It was the rusty pile of scrap he'd seen downtown the day before.

Ace was home.

This was the guy who'd set him up, who'd endangered his family, and who'd killed at least three people in cold blood. Jake wasn't about to knock politely. Not when he had a better idea.

Harley had said Ace lived with his mother, and if the punk didn't work, someone had to pay the bills. Jake was betting Ace's mother was at work, and the lazy punk was home alone.

It was time to find out.

And if his dangerous plan didn't work, Jake could be in a bigger mess than he already was.

He stepped onto the unsteady deck at the rear of the house and faced a door. It was locked, and he decided after this, he might get Annie to show him how to pick a lock. But for now, he had no choice but to use brute force.

It wouldn't need a lot of effort. The lock was old, the frame was rotting, and he was determined.

He was already wanted for murder, so what harm could a little illegal entry do?

Jake put his shoulder to the door, braced his feet, and

pushed. He felt it give. This was gonna be a breeze. He pushed harder and wood crackled, groaned, and the door gave way.

Then a security chain stopped it.

Nothing but a minor annoyance.

He braced himself again, tensed his leg muscles, and pushed. The chain broke free and the door burst open. He grabbed the knob and stopped the door from crashing backwards into the wall, then stepped into the kitchen.

CHAPTER 42

Friday, 9:43 a.m.

ANNIE HURRIED across the precinct floor and dropped into the guest chair at Hank's desk. The cop looked up as she slid an envelope toward him. "I need you to find out who this is ASAP," she said.

"Good morning, Annie," Hank said. "Nice to see you, too." He picked up the envelope and slipped out the photo. "Who's this?"

"It's Ace."

Hank raised an eyebrow. "The guy who tried to run you off the road?"

"Yes."

Hank gave Annie a dubious look. "Where'd you get this?"

"He was at Merrilla Overstone's wake. Lisa gave it to me."

Hank frowned. "What's this guy's connection to all this?"

"He's not only the guy who tried to kill Matty and me, but

I believe he's the man who robbed the bank, shot Mrs. Overstone, and tried to kill Niles Overstone."

Hank whistled and squinted at the photo. "He does look a lot like Jake."

"Can you find out who he is?"

"We'll run it through facial rec. If he's in the system, we'll soon see." Hank spun his chair around and rolled over to Callaway's desk, then beckoned toward Annie a moment later.

Annie went over and sat across from the young cop. The photo of Ace lay on the desk, and Callaway pointed to it. "I'll run that in a minute, but I have something to show you first."

He turned his monitor so Annie and Hank could see. "I was able to recover some pictures from the memory card," he said. "The card's rather fragmented. You've been using it for a while, but the most recent pictures were almost all fully recoverable."

Hank and Annie leaned forward, their eyes on the monitor.

Callaway tapped a key and a directory of photo icons appeared. "These all have a timestamp from this Tuesday. I assume that's what you're interested in, Hank?"

"Yes."

"This is the earliest one," Callaway said, double-clicking an icon. A shot of a man approaching the driveway of a house appeared on the screen. Taken from a distance away, only a partial side view of the man's face was visible.

"That's the Overstone house," Annie said, pointing at the monitor. "And that's Ace."

"It could be him," Hank said calmly. "But it's not very clear from this distance. Can you zoom in?"

Annie looked at Hank. She could tell he was pleased to see the photos, but the cop was holding back his elation.

Callaway zoomed in. What was visible of the face was in the shadow of a baseball cap, and the features were unclear. They went through the other photos, one by one. Close-up shots had been taken as well, but the man's back had been turned to the camera.

Hank sat back. "Cue up the bank video again, Callaway. I wanna see the best shot you can get me of the guy's face."

In a moment, Annie squinted at a blurry still of the bank robber. She compared it to the shots from the camera and the photo of Ace.

"All three photos are of the same man," she said, pointing to the screen. "And in the picture at the house, he's still wearing the same clothes he had on at the bank robbery."

Hank turned to Annie and gave her the thumbs-up. His smile turned to a grin. "As unclear as they are, the existence of these photos is the best news I've had all week."

Annie sat back and gave Hank a smug look. "Jake wasn't lying to you."

The cop's eyes twinkled. "So it appears."

"And now you're convinced he's innocent?"

"Totally convinced. But who erased the pictures?"

Annie held up the photo of Ace. "He did. After he shot Mrs. Overstone, he left through the basement window and went to the car. Then he deleted the photos and planted the cell phone." She paused. "And Jake's out there somewhere looking for him."

Hank rubbed at his chin. "First we need to find out who he is. Then we can bring him in and talk to him."

"I'll get on it right now," Callaway said, taking the photo from Annie. "Shouldn't take too long."

Annie followed Hank back to his desk and they sat down.

"We still have a problem," Hank said. "I've never been more pleased in my life than I am to see those photos. It proves Jake was telling the truth. But we still have no proof it's Ace in the video or at the house. They're not clear enough, and as far as a jury would be concerned, it could be Jake."

"So how do we prove it's Ace and not Jake?"

"Other than a confession, I don't know." He paused. "With your testimony, there's no doubt we can get him for trying to run you off the road. Officers are out there right now following up on all the registered red Mustangs in the area, but there're a lot of them. So far, they've had no luck. But once we find the Mustang, we should have proof of the hit and run. But at the moment, that's all we have. A charge of him shooting off a firearm wouldn't likely stick, especially with no evidence he fired it."

"What about Jake's testimony?"

Hank shook his head. "Jake's still officially a suspect. His word is worthless without proof. With the evidence against him, it would look like he's making up a story to cover himself."

"And the photos?" Annie asked.

Hank shrugged. "Any good lawyer could argue the time on the camera might've been changed and the photos taken earlier, perhaps photos of Jake taken by you."

"That doesn't make any sense."

"Along with everything else, it could help convince a jury of Jake's guilt."

Annie blew out an exasperated sigh. She had no doubt Ace was behind everything, but their hands were tied.

"Sorry, Annie. I'm still not free to do anything to help Jake. And Diego wants him brought in ASAP."

"Hank." It was Callaway calling. "I've got an ID on this guy."

Annie and Hank hurried over to Callaway's desk.

"His name's Albert Irish," the young cop said. "Twenty-four years old. He's got a short record. Been in prison a couple of times for break and enter."

Hank leaned in and looked at the monitor.

Callaway continued, "He has a red 2007 Mustang registered in his name."

"Address?"

"Two twenty Crestwood Avenue."

Hank looked at Annie. "We can bring him in and talk to him. But again, all we have is the hit and run, and it's up to you to press charges."

Hank seemed to be leaving the decision up to her, and she didn't know what to say. If she pressed charges, they'd bring Ace in. But once he was in custody, Annie feared he'd clam up as soon as they questioned him further. And if he got a lawyer, the lack of evidence against Ace wouldn't do Jake any good. Ace would receive little more than a slap on the wrist.

"Hank, there's more," Callaway said. "Got some family info on Irish. His mother was remarried some time ago, then divorced again. She still goes by her most recent married name of Tinker."

"Tinker?" Annie said. "How do I know that name?"

Callaway sat back and looked at Annie. "Wanda Tinker is Merrilla Overstone's sister."

Annie's eyes widened. "That means Ace Irish is Merrilla Overstone's nephew."

CHAPTER 43

Friday, 9:57 a.m.

JAKE HAD SPENT the last few minutes becoming familiar with the layout of the house. First, he'd made sure Ace's mother wasn't in the kitchen or living room, then he'd crept down the short hallway to a pair of bedrooms.

The first one, a woman's room, had been empty.

And now, as he stood in front of the other room, where soft snoring sounds came from behind the closed bedroom door, he hoped his foolish plan would work.

He took a deep breath, turned the knob, and pushed the door open.

A man lay on the bed facing away. He groaned, rolled onto his back and stretched. Then he turned his head and looked at Jake.

The man's mouth fell open, his eyes enlarged, and he sprang to a sitting position. One hand reached for the drawer of a stand beside his bed.

Jake waited patiently in the doorway while Ace fumbled in the drawer and removed a pistol. He pointed it toward Jake, gazing down the barrel with unfocused eyes.

"The police are outside," Jake said. "You'd better be careful with that thing."

Ace looked at the weapon, then toward the bedroom window facing the rear of the house, then back at Jake. He frowned. "So why didn't they come in?"

"They're waiting for a warrant. They plan to arrest you for trying to run my wife off the road. I'm the only one who knows what else you did, and I'm here to talk to you."

Ace glanced at his gun, then gave a short laugh. "I don't see what good talk is gonna do. I'm the one with the gun."

"If you kill me, that'll make four murders," Jake said. "Are you prepared to handle that?"

Ace narrowed his eyes. "If I shoot you, it's for breaking into my house. There's no way they can prove I shot anyone else." He smiled. "I set you up too good. The cops think you killed all those people."

Jake laughed. "Here's the thing, Ace. The police know I'm in here, so if you kill me, it's murder."

Ace struggled to pull a pair of pants on with one hand, then managed to work a t-shirt over his head. He slipped on a pair of running shoes, then, keeping one eye on Jake, he went to the window. He peered out and looked around, then turned back and motioned with the pistol. "Into the living room."

Jake turned and went into the hallway. Ace followed, prodding him into the living room. Then, going to the front window, he pulled the drapes slightly aside and looked outside. He turned back with a frown. "There're no cops out there."

"All right," Jake said. "You got me. I just didn't want you to shoot me until we had a chance to talk."

"Doesn't matter," Ace said. "I'm gonna kill you, anyway. Just not here. Not in my mother's house."

Jake crossed his arms. "You don't have to kill me, Ace. I'll make a deal with you. Give me the money from the bank robbery and everybody's happy."

Ace glared a moment, a deep frown on his face. "Couldn't do it if I wanted to. The money's gone. You know that. Hicks put most of it in your garage."

Jake shrugged. "Then give me what's left."

"I spent it."

Jake sighed. "I'm trying to help you out here."

"No. You're trying to blackmail me."

"Yeah, you could call it that. I say it's splitting the profits. I need a little something to get out of town." Jake shrugged. "You did a number on me, and I have no choice."

"I got no money."

"What about Merrilla Overstone?" Jake asked. "Didn't you get anything from her?"

"I will soon, but not yet."

"How soon."

"Once I get rid of Uncle Niles."

Uncle Niles? What was Ace talking about?

"Are you telling me Merrilla Overstone is your aunt?" Jake asked.

Ace nodded.

"So how much money can you get me?" Jake said. "I need ten grand."

Ace shrugged. "Hafta wait for the insurance. Might take a few days." He narrowed his eyes. "I still think it'd be easier to kill you and be done with it."

"And mar your perfect record?"

Ace laughed. "Yeah, it all worked out pretty well."

"Look," Jake said, "I'm willing to shake on this deal if you are. I have a safe place to go, but I need some money. Maybe I can work for you after this all blows over."

"Don't know as I need anybody else. And you're too hot." He looked around the room, scratching his head. Finally, he continued, "But I'll help you out on one condition."

"What's that?"

"I need you to kill Niles Overstone."

"Why?"

"Once he's dead, the insurance money goes to my mother. Then I'll have access to it. Uncle Niles has no family, and neither did Auntie." He laughed. "It's not exactly the way Auntie planned it, but it works for me."

"Your aunt wanted your uncle dead?" Jake asked.

"Don't be an idiot. Of course not. She wanted him to get the insurance money and help me out at the same time."

"Help you out how?"

Ace sighed. "She knew I robbed the bank. She said she recognized me when my mask fell off, and she cornered me. Said if I help her out, she won't turn me in. She figured the cops would find a connection between me and her eventually, so I had nothing to lose and lots to gain."

"So you were happy to oblige."

Ace shrugged. "Once I found out the bills were marked, and I wouldn't be able to spend the money, she had me over a barrel. So what could I do? Besides, when she told me she'd left five grand to me in her will, I was all ears. So we talked a little more, and we finally came up with a simple plan."

"It was an amazing plan, Ace. I have to hand it to you," Jake said, then laughed. "But why kill your aunt?"

"That was the whole idea. She really wanted to die in the worst way. Had cancer, you know. Said she would've killed herself, but she wanted to make sure my uncle got the insurance money." He shrugged. "Apparently, they don't pay for suicide. It was a good plan, though. One where no one would think my uncle was involved. She wanted to make sure he wasn't suspected in any way. But I changed the plan a little bit after I got to thinking about all the money."

"You're a genius, Ace," Jake said.

Ace puffed up his chest. "Yeah, I guess I am." He had his arms crossed now, the pistol relaxed and pointing to the side. "Auntie chickened out at the last minute, though. I don't think she really thought it through before. Once she saw my gun, she changed her mind and started to shake all over, begging me not to continue." He sighed. "Hated to do it after that, but, you know. She can't wave money in front of me like that and then change her mind. It ain't fair."

"You're absolutely right, Ace," Jake said. "It wasn't fair at all. But why frame me?"

Ace laughed. "Some people think we look alike. Auntie did too. Said she saw you on the news. After we started tossing around ideas, I came up with the plan to set you up. Auntie thought it was a great idea, because anyone who saw me at the bank would swear it was you after the cops started mentioning your name around. She called it the power of suggestion or something like that."

"Amazing plan, Ace."

Ace continued, "She told you my uncle was having an affair and hired you to watch the house. All I had to do was come to the house, shoot her, then sneak out the basement window and plant the phone in your car. She'd arranged all the phone calls and text messages already, so I didn't have to worry about none of that."

"And the camera?"

"We didn't think about any camera, but when I saw it, I was gonna take it. Then, I figured if you took any shots, it would be better to erase them and leave the camera there."

"What about the woman next door?"

Ace shrugged. "According to Auntie, that snoopy woman's always in the backyard. She'd be sure to hear the shot. And we opened the back door so you'd think I ran out there. We didn't know you'd grab the gun and run outside with it, so that was a bonus. Got your prints on the gun and the woman saw you holding it. And voila. A simple and perfect setup."

"Yes, it was perfect," Jake said. "But what if your aunt had lived?"

Ace roared with laughter. "That was a bad shot. The plan was to shoot her in the heart. But like I said, Auntie changed her mind, and she was struggling so much, I shot her in the wrong spot. The poor woman had to go through a bit of pain." He shrugged. "But it all worked out in the end. Actually, it worked out better than all right. Auntie lived long enough to tell the cops it was you who shot her. With your prints on the gun, who was gonna doubt that?"

"You nailed me good, Ace," Jake said. "I admire you for that." He held out a hand. "So, do we have a deal?"

Ace looked at the outstretched hand.

Jake took a step forward. "We have to shake on it."

Ace frowned and brought his gun hand around, pointing the weapon at Jake. "Not so fast."

Jake lunged forward, reaching for the gun.

CHAPTER 44

Friday, 10:14 a.m.

ANNIE SAT IN THE backseat of Hank's car as it sped toward 220 Crestwood. King was holding Hank's cell, and she leaned forward, listening in alarm as sounds of a battle came over the phone.

A few minutes earlier, following the revelation Ace was Merrilla Overstone's nephew, Hank had decided it was reason enough to bring Ace in for a good long talk. Annie had insisted on coming along.

"If you don't, I'm going to follow in my car, and you can't stop me," she'd stubbornly said.

Hank had relented.

Halfway to their destination, Hank's cell phone had rung, and he'd been surprised to hear Jake's voice. The moment he'd found out what was transpiring, he'd set the phone to record the call, then put it on speaker. They'd listened to Ace's entire confession.

But now, something other than talk was going on inside the house.

"We'd better get there before Jake gets himself shot," King said. He'd been fingering his weapon the whole time, and he looked ready to charge in the moment they reached the house.

The portable police siren blared from its spot on the roof. Cars pulled over in front of them. Hank leaned into the steering wheel and spun around a vehicle that had failed to yield.

Backup was on the way, but he was eager to get there before it was too late.

Amid grunts and thumps, Jake's voice sounded from the phone. "I hope you're on your way, Hank."

Then, the sound of a single gunshot came over the line, and Annie held her breath.

"I'm okay," Jake said a moment later. "But he's getting away. He crashed right through the back window."

Hank spun the vehicle onto Crestwood Drive, and King pointed. "Two twenty."

The vehicle ground to a stop and the cops jumped out.

"Annie, you stay here," Hank called over his shoulder.

Hank ran toward the front door of the house as King circled around behind.

An engine roared from the rear of the building. It was the Mustang.

Annie leaped over the seat and worked her way behind the steering wheel. She started the car, hit the gas, and backed the Chevy into the driveway. It stopped at an awkward angle, blocking the exit.

She spun around in her seat and held her breath as the Mustang thundered toward her. The Chevy rocked as the other vehicle rammed its bumper. Then the Mustang howled and leaped off the driveway onto the front lawn.

Hank leveled his weapon and fired two shots as the powerful car lurched over the sidewalk and hit the street.

Jake raced out the front door of the house and stopped beside Hank. King appeared from behind, emptying his weapon at the fleeing vehicle.

The rear tire of the Mustang exploded, and the vehicle careened off the street. It continued for a hundred feet, one wheel on the sidewalk, as the driver fought to bring it under control. Then the Mustang sideswiped a tree and came to a shattering stop, its front end damaged beyond repair against a second immovable tree.

Ace leaped from the vehicle and sprinted up the street in the opposite direction.

Jake and the two cops raced after the fugitive, but Ace had a long lead.

He was getting away.

Annie had no choice.

She dropped the Chevy into gear and hit the gas. Tires whined as the vehicle hurtled onto the street and gathered speed. She zoomed past the detectives and clung to the steering wheel, gaining on the fleeing man.

Jake had outraced the cops and was twenty feet ahead of Hank. He turned and stepped aside as the Chevy approached. Jake had a big grin on his face and one thumb in the air when Annie whipped past him.

She was closing in. Ace glanced over his shoulder, then veered left and crossed the sidewalk, heading for a pathway between two houses.

Annie didn't let up. She gave the steering wheel a hard wrench. Her head brushed the ceiling as the Chevy lurched wildly and bounced over the curb. It spun onto the front lawn of the house, its front end almost on the heels of the fugitive.

With one smooth motion, Annie slammed on the brakes, threw the car into park, and opened the driver-side door. She sprang from the vehicle and hit the ground running.

Ace was fast, but he was tiring, panting for air as Annie closed in.

Two feet from the killer, she dove forward and tackled the runner. She wrapped her arms around his legs, clinging with all she had.

They both went down. Her breath left her body with a whoosh as his foot dug into her ribs.

He cursed and she hung on, but he was slipping from her grasp.

Just a few more seconds and Jake would be there.

Just a few more seconds.

Ace worked one leg loose and kicked frantically. His heel caught her in the shoulder, and she felt an intense pain. Her arms grew weak. She lost her grip, now clinging to one ankle with both hands.

He struggled, kicked, and cursed. Then, with a final desperate heave, he worked his foot free, and Annie was left holding a running shoe. She tossed it aside in disgust, then lay prostrate, exhausted, and too tired to persevere. From the corner of her eye, she saw the killer roll to his feet and stumble away.

Then a blur ran past, leaped forward, and brought the fugitive to the ground.

It was Jake.

Annie struggled to her feet, a bruised rib causing her to wince in pain, but with an expression of triumph on her face.

Ace lay prone on the ground, one arm wrenched behind his back. He struggled in vain as the full weight of Jake's body held him down.

Handcuffs rattled as Hank knelt and cuffed the defeated fugitive, then Jake stepped back as the detectives dragged the sputtering man to his feet and read him his rights.

Without a word, Jake put his arm around Annie and drew her close. She was exhausted and sore all over, but it didn't matter. She was happy.

Jake was coming home at last.

EPILOGUE

Friday, 3:10 p.m.

HANK FOLDED UP his notes and stepped back from the podium. The hastily assembled press conference had gone well, and he'd been able to answer most of the questions put to him.

The subject of Jake's once-suspected involvement hadn't come up. Instead, he'd made sure the press knew the Lincolns deserved the credit for breaking the case wide open.

As the crowd of reporters dissipated, he turned to Jake and Annie and flashed a grin. He'd never before been so pleased at the outcome of a case, and his face couldn't stop showing it.

They went back into the precinct, and the three of them sat around Hank's desk. He had a pile of paperwork to take care of, interviews to do, and statements to take.

It was going to be a long process, but it could wait.

"Ace's confession is what really nailed this case closed," Hank said, looking at Jake. "Once he found out there'd been an open phone line, and we'd heard his confession, he knew he was sunk."

"Did he confess to killing Dewey Hicks?" Annie asked. "I don't think Jake managed to get that out of him."

Hank nodded. "Yes, he did. We're gonna be having a few more long talks with him, but everything he told us appears to fit together with what we already knew and with Jake's story."

"What about the insurance money?" Jake asked.

Hank shrugged. "I'm no expert in that area. But usually, a death benefit won't be paid if the insured commits suicide. Niles Overstone might have to fight for it, but since the policy was a few years old, he might stand a chance of winning."

"Ace was an idiot," Jake said. "If Niles Overstone was dead, it doesn't mean the money would go to Wanda Tinker. We don't know what Niles has in his will. He might be leaving everything to charity."

"Ace isn't very bright, anyway," Annie said. "Jake had him fooled pretty easily."

Jake frowned at Annie. "Are you saying my brilliant plan wasn't all that brilliant?"

Annie laughed. "It was a little hairy."

"It worked. That's the main thing," Jake said with a shrug. "Besides, I didn't have much choice."

"Diego's happy about how it all worked out," Hank said. "He wouldn't admit it, but I think he's feeling a little guilty about not giving you more support."

"I won't hold it against him," Jake said. "That is, unless I need some leverage in the future."

"I have a lot of sympathy for Niles Overstone," Hank said. "When he heard what his wife had planned, he took it hard. Eventually he revealed she hadn't been herself lately. Her emotions had run from one extreme to the other, from fear of dying to looking forward to it. Though Niles had tried to convince her otherwise, Merrilla's greatest concern was in being a burden to her husband in her final few days."

"I guess I can forgive her for trying to frame me," Jake said. "Actually, I blame Ace for coming up with the idea and taking advantage of his aunt's fragile physical and mental condition."

"When all is said and done," Hank said, "we can't forget the woman killed at the bank, Arlina Madine." He paused and sighed. "I need to visit her family yet. They'll be pleased the murderer has been caught. A small consolation, but it's something."

Annie looked at her watch. "We'd better be getting home. Matty'll be there soon, and he'll be looking forward to seeing his daddy."

"And his daddy's looking forward to seeing him," Jake said as he stood. "I have to tell him how brave his mother was."

Annie laughed and stood. "Yeah, I was so busy being brave, no one noticed I was scared to death."

Hank sat back, chuckling to himself as he watched his good friends leave. The case was closed, and he'd be able to relax for a while.

He picked up his briefcase, flipped it open, and removed the small velvet-covered box.

He had no excuses left, and he had some plans to make.

###

CPSIA information can be obtained
at www.ICGtesting.com
Printed in the USA
LVOW12s2317080916
503852LV00004B/167/P